THE RED LION
FISH PARADOX

And Other Stories

John Corral

ISBN-13: 9798433439153
ISBN-10: 1477123456

Cover design by: Art Painter
Library of Congress Control Number: 2018675309
Printed in the United States of America

To Tanya

"Genius is relative. If you judge a fish by its ability to climb a tree, it will live its whole life believing that it is stupid."

--ALBERT EINSTEIN

CONTENTS

PREFACE

From his many well-received collections of short stories, John Corral has gained a reputation as one of the best short fiction writers on amazon.com. As one reviewer noted, "He raises ordinary people and everyday occurences to a new height, exploring and infusing them with new meaning." This new collection of stories, most of them originally published in online magazines over the last decade, adds to his reputation.

In the title story, *The Red Lion Fish Paradox*, a newly minted Enviremental Studies Ph.D. graduate tries her hand at actual work with surprising results. And in several theme linked stories that follow, the connection between the narrator and the main characters tends to blur and unfold in telling and often insightful vignettes. Of their time and yet timeless, Corral's stories zero in on everyday life with wit, candor, grace, and an acurately observant eye.

AT HOME

It was the first time we stopped in the town of Clear Lake, though we'd seen the signs for it a few times when hiking nearby. We pulled over at one of those shabby general stores you still see in rural areas.

The place had a large frontage with a porch sagging under the weight of a rusty soda vending machine. There was a second-story apartment above the store, this one with two sash windows overlooking the tin roof above the porch, lace curtains brown with age, and, I swear, there was even a kerosene lantern glowing in one window up there.

I shook my head. Didn't they have electricity in this place? Were we that far back in the woods?

I had a funny feeling of deja vu. I glanced up and saw the lantern flickering, and a face of a girl appeared for a brief moment, no longer, I'm sure of it, as I got out my side of the SUV after we parked. It was just as dusk was settling in, the woods thick and already moss-black behind the red clapboard building. It was late September, and I could feel a chill in the air.

I tugged at my sports bra through my cycling jersey to bring a cool breeze to my skin under the damp fabric. I could hear the sound of running water coming from somewhere, maybe a spring or a creek in the woods, behind the store. Otherwise, it was quiet, just the engine ticking as it cooled.

Todd saw to the bikes, checking once more that they were secure on the roof of the SUV, the trusty old Toyota 4Runner he'd bought off his brother, a gas guzzler I told him we'd have to trade for a Prius, or something at least environmentally sane, once we paid off the expenses from our wedding. (I knew he didn't want to give it up, even though he agreed it was a real planet killer.)

We'd just put in a hard day on trails through the Sierra wilderness. I'd fallen on a tight cutback, a downhill washout with stair-step ledges strewn with smooth baby-head stones, and I'd cut my shin, a pretty good laceration.

I was lucky, I knew—I could easily have broken something in the fall—but the pain brought tears to my eyes. I hoped the store might have some alcohol wipes or iodine, gauze pads; I'd somehow forgotten to pack the first aid kit.

I opened the screen door and limped into a room as wide as the building itself and about as deep, the aisles too narrow, shelves too close together but sparsely stocked, my shin throbbing, raw where the skin opened almost to bone—I could only stand to take a quick, clinical look—and it stung where air met the wound.

A bell tinkled as I teetered in my cleats on floorboards that looked worn and warped as the deck of an old sailing vessel, buckling up in places, tricky to navigate. Seeing no one tending the cash register at the back of the store, I called out a hello. No answer.

A pair of moose or elk antlers that looked about twelve feet across hung on the back wall, mounted to a stained board, dark with age, and below them were a few smaller trophies—the head of a deer, what looked like a boar's head—and some framed black-and-whites of men standing next to their kills, guns casually angled from the crooks of their arms toward the ground.

To my right, just inside the door, hanging from a nail in a post supporting the story above, I caught my reflection in a small mirror at the top of one of those old-time thermometers advertising some extinct soda or remedy.

I hadn't put on any lipstick, and in the fading light, my lips looked green, my face the sallow color of a dead woman. I felt a strange shock, a snap of adrenaline, as if I were looking at a wax effigy of myself, everything exaggerated, a little hurtful.

Even when I tried to dispel the odd sensation by smiling—my gapped front teeth showing between those green lips when my mirror image smiled in response—some other version of myself, some nightmare or practical joke held me in its gaze.

I closed my eyes, and when I opened them, the face I reflected looked calm, serene, at home in this place. I appraised my vision as if it were someone else: mouth too wide, chin too pointy, dark rings under the eyes like some poor girl in a vampire movie from the '20s. This is Fiona, I said to her. I repeated, Fiona, as if to give new life to my own name. But the reflected person didn't seem to hear.

What I saw, looking at her as if for the first time, was a woman turned twenty-six the day before, dark hair gray along the part above her left eye, built small, delicate boned, small-breasted, sweat rings under the armpits of her pale-blue cycling jersey, possibly pregnant but not yet showing, in one hand a purple nylon wallet that wouldn't prove much use in this place.

"Todd?" I called out the door behind me, "I'm just going to see if they have some water."

I didn't know why I said that. Todd already knew why I went into the store. Who did I want to hear that I had a man with me? Was it fear I felt, dread of the unknown, or something else? I couldn't quite tell. It was the same feeling I experienced years ago in a class on ethics, when I had to stand for 40 minutes while a professor ripped my ego and confidence to shreds because I dared question her on her interpretation of what Socrates once said about the difference between knowledge and wisdom.

I almost dropped out of college after that, and only talked out of it by a counselor who said experiences like that were intended to toughen you, not make you quit. Remembering that advise, I stepped forward, heartened and resolved.

First aid supplies did not seem a category of goods the store would carry, judging from what was displayed. I couldn't be sure anything had been restocked or dusted since Clinton's inauguration.

Before I turned back to search further in the store, I saw my husband pulling a pair of jeans on over his biking shorts, his ass squared against a truck's fender for balance. I had no idea what would happen next, no idea it was already happening.

I remember thinking how vain he was, not wanting to be seen in bike shorts; it was something I never understood with him. (Maybe he thought I should wear makeup when we went trail riding in the woods; I never thought to ask.)

Sure, I could have changed out of my cleats into my sneakers in the truck—we were done for the day—but I, for one, didn't mind walking into a store and looking a little silly, unlike Todd.

I guess if someone were to chase me, I wouldn't get very far, but that was not a thought in my head, even if I was feeling a little spooked, standing just inside the door of this rickety old building, listening for another human being, hearing only the sound of a clock ticking off the exact second as if each were a solid year: tock . . . tock . . . tock . . .

"Hello?" I called out again. This time I heard something, if not a response, a kind of clumping and dragging sound. Someone moving an old, heavy trunk? The sound came from beyond the back wall, or maybe from upstairs; I couldn't quite tell.

I looked around what I could see of the store for a cooler, thinking if they had one, that's where I could find a couple of bottles of water to clean up my shin and for the ride down the mountain and the long drive back to Sacramento. I could leave a few dollars on the counter and go. The shin hurt when I put weight on it, a deep ache, but nothing was broken, I could tell.

Then I heard the 4Runner start up outside—a chuff of a misfire, then a roar—and in the same instant, I saw a man in front of me, seated on a stool behind the counter, where no one had been the split second before.

What had changed? I realized the overhead fluorescent tubes had flickered on, dim, buzzing, emitting a tired stain more green smoke than light; I couldn't see the man's eyes for the reflection of the long fixtures in his glasses, the lenses large and square, tinted a tea color, the green bars reflected in them seeming a kind of cage he was content to sit inside. His hair was olive in the light, flown to one side, his face peppered with dark spots and acne divots.

He sat like an Indian chief, I thought, or at least he could have been part Native American; he sat so still, impassive in his brown-plaid shirt as though he'd been there for hours. (I don't know why I thought he looked like an Indian; I try not to see color. Christ, I went to Berkeley!) He might have been smiling, but with another part of my mind, I was still trying to figure out why Todd had started the truck, even as I heard the tires spit gravel.

A moment of confusion, bewilderment, isolation. I contracted as if I was a turtle pulling my head and legs into my shell. I could feel myself shrink into myself. Then weightlessness, I felt as though I were floating, unattached to earth. That feeling hit with the hor-rible out-of-body certainty that Todd was leaving me here, alone. He was going and leaving me. It came to me that he had never loved me. (When had he said he loved me last? When had he ever expressed so without my prompting?)

I knew why he would leave me, of course, even as it came to me that he would return and that, in his way, he did love me, but im-perious attachment was all he could muster, and it might not be enough.

The feeling passed in the course of a few steady, slow breaths. Like it does when I awaken from a disturbing dream, turn on the bedside light, and read a chapter of something or just scroll my Twitter feed. Maybe my anal husband was just headed to find a spot to turn the truck around, I told myself, so we'd be heading in the right direction when I came out of the store. Still, there remained a slight nick of pain at the back of my skull, the sparking of a synapse that stung, akin to the feel of the point of a knife on bone.

I walked down the narrow aisle between the sparse canned goods and rolls of flypaper, past mousetraps and Hershey cocoa in tins, thinking in a strange way of what it would be like to live up here—not so far from civilization, after all, but so remote—and asked the man whether he had any bottled water. My wallet was in my hand, level with and resting on my collarbone.

He was smiling now, a warm smile, not a sneer as it had seemed to me at first from the front of the store, that tell of slight revulsion country folk sometimes just can't help but show toward city people. He made a gentle bow as he rose from his stool and put his hand up. He wouldn't take money. He turned his back to me and lifted a mason jar from a wooden case of jars with metal lids that sat on the shelf right behind his place at the counter. He unscrewed the cap and poured from the jar into a paper cup.

I was about to protest, say something, and I was even a little affronted he thought I didn't have the cash to pay for Poland Spring or whatever they sold up here on the mountain. Still, my hand closed around the cup he offered, a wax cup with a pattern circling just below the rim, a meandering vine with alternating heart-shaped leaves, infinitely looping, a kind of horizontal tree of life. I realized how thirsty I was, which the moment before I thought was just dry mouth from my fit of anger on account of Todd.

The water was silver and seemed to gather all the light in the room and clean it, even the murk of the fluorescent. The room seemed to exist upside down inside the cup of water; a miniature 3D model is the way it looked, rather than just a reflection. I glanced up and could see the man's eyes. I studied him. He looked kind, if a little sad. I decided I could trust him—no reason not to—and I drank the water, which felt like time itself flowing right into my veins. Was I that dehydrated from the mountain biking?

"Thank you," I said. I put the cup down on the counter. I tried to think what I could buy, some small thing, a token. There were baseball cards, a quaint and very old dispenser for Lifesavers, and a box of those little kits in glass vials, for fixing broken glasses. The selections were limited.

I bought two postcards, both black-and-white: one of a pair of women, maybe from the 1950s, in tennis outfits of that era, holding wooden rackets; the other of an octagonal meeting house or perhaps a church or school; a group of small children lined up along the front and not smiling.

The shopkeeper made change. Two postcards for a quarter; they would have been a dollar each at the inn we'd just checked out of down the hill.

"So, better?" he said. If he was Native American, he had a Spanish accent. "Should heal quick." He moved the back of his hand from the counter in a broad gesture meant to include my shin, my whole being, maybe.

"Spring water. Natural medicine," he said. "It heals anything." He refilled the cup, then bowed his head, or instead tipped it down, raising it again a moment later, almost a slow, two-part nod. I tipped some of the water onto a paper napkin I took from a stack on the counter and held it over the wound on my shin. What I felt was pure relief. My body flooded with it, a sensation like floating in a warm, calm sea.

I had a ridiculous thought at that moment, an idea so zany I completely forgot about it almost as I had it, though the relief lasted beyond my forgetting: it wasn't Todd's child I was carrying. I tipped my head back and drained the cup. I felt the water gather inside my lower lip, pass through my teeth, then a cool stream ran along either side of my tongue on its way down my throat.

There had been some blood—even the beginnings of an ugly scab over what surely would become a scar an inch long—but when I gently removed the napkin to look, the wound seemed much smaller than I remembered. Hardly a nick, really. Could it have healed together like that so quickly? My shinbone still throbbed a little when I put weight on it, but the pain was nearly gone. I could have gone dancing, and danced the night away. Maybe I had only been focusing too much on my guilt before, how I was a burden to Todd, slowing him down.

Maybe it was right of him to leave me behind.

Then my mind darkened once again as I remembered something I was not proud of. It happened every few days, more often now than before. It concerns Todd's younger brother, Peter.

I was carrying my wedding dress down the hall to the room where I was supposed to change. The photographer had texted me three or four times by now, though I wasn't running late. The bridesmaids were all there, three of them already drunk enough at breakfast that I knew I had to read them the riot act about not spoiling my wedding day. No way were they to humiliate me in front of my parents, family members, and friends with schoolgirl antics. Clutching my dress, I could feel the tension between my eyebrows, just above my nose.

I forced myself to smile and relax my forehead when I passed my aunt and uncle from Nebraska in the hall. He wore seersucker— the only man left in North America who could pull off such a suit; it was June, and it was balmy—and she wore a pale-blue dress with a brooch that was either a unicorn or a carousel pony; whichever, it seemed vaguely religious, its front legs intersecting as if it was making a sign of the cross.

I was going to give my bridesmaids a lecture, or else I would just suck it up. I hadn't decided which way to go when I ran into Peter. I ran into him so hard a button popped off his vest and rolled along the carpet like a tiny lost hubcap. He'd stepped out of his room right into my path, and I was going full stride. He apologized and cupped my elbow in his hand, ready to catch me, I guess, if I was going to spin out of control and crash.

"Don't do this," he said.

I tracked the button to see it tip and fall beside the baseboard at the edge of the carpet runner, then I put my hand on his arm and looked at him. Half his face was covered in shaving cream, the other half clean-shaven, just thin strips of the white foam across his cheek. He looked as though he'd been crying, his skin puffy, his eyes red. His hair—short curls, brown—was receding; I'd never noticed that before. I also remember thinking he must have heard me coming. How can someone know another person's walk? What does that even take?

"Call this off. Take some time," he said. "Talk to me." I heard my phone ding: another text from the photographer.

"Peter, it's too late," I think I told him, "we are not doing this now." Yes, I had slept with him. It was the summer before, and as far as I knew, he had never told Todd, but I was slightly anxious about it, especially now that he was holding onto me in a way I didn't like, his fingers pressing into my wrists. I had a moment of thinking if he didn't let me go, I wouldn't be able to get away. He could drag me into his room. He was strong; he had a wrestler's body, unlike Todd, who was slender and a runner.

"Look," I said, "I've been thinking about it too, but this is not the time. Don't worry," I think I said—"trust me, Pete."

Anyway, I got away, which is all I wanted at that instant. I remember having the powerful wish that something would happen, something open up for him—even if it was a disaster on its face. But if it set him free, turned him in a new direction, he would be better for it. My mind raced through my bridesmaids' faces with real animus, willing just one of them to get him drunk and take him to bed (after the ceremony, of course).

He wasn't Todd's best man. There was always some kind of friction between them. I remember seeing Peter at the back of the small church, standing, bolts of the late-afternoon light streaming through the doors from outside and glowing golden in his brown curls. He turned and left before the ceremony was over. He was there, and then he was not. Just a beam of sunlight sparkling in swirling motes of dust remained where he'd stood—particles of him. I would see him again. I promised myself.

I did seek him out one week after I returned from my honeymoon. And, yes, we did it. One last time, we both said.

Todd blasted past the store. I turned—I guess I must have heard the throaty exhaust and the high-transmission whine the SUV made, the rumble of its all-terrain tires—just in time to see through the plate-glass windows the taillights of the 4Runner streak past the front of the store, the day outside now full twilight. How could he? Later I would understand, but at that moment, I hated him. I suppose at that moment I was sure he had found out, that Pete had told him about us.

Whether it was anger or shame I felt—or which had the upper hand in the battle raging inside me—I couldn't say. What does it matter? I tried to reassure myself. Yet I knew I was scared. Scared? No, terrified of having to do what I knew must be done—to tell Todd, even if Peter hadn't. Or there couldn't be any point in going on.

Todd was consistent, reliable to a fault. Rigid. Forgiveness—if it were possible—would come in the form of a mathematical equation; he wasn't the type to talk it out, let alone indulge in therapy. My fear turned to rapid and profound fatigue.

There was an overstuffed armchair in the corner of the store, just past the end of the counter, set at an angle in a nook, complete with that old-school funny white piece of a lacy towel over the headrest. A potbelly stove was next to it, planted there like a prop from a TV show about Norman Rockwell.

Where am I? How did I get here? I couldn't think. I just went for the chair, sleep overtaking me as I fell into it. Minutes or hours later, I felt someone tugging at my bicycle shoes—one, then the other—removing them from my feet. I slipped back under without opening my eyes.

I remember when I first met Death. We had a wordless conversation. We lived on a farm when I was a child. It was just outside a small Midwestern city plopped amid cornfields and oil wells. My father and mother both taught in the university's music department; they were one-half of a distinguished string quartet that performed in all the capitals of Europe and worldwide.

Our farm was woods and hills and rolling fields, though the land just to the north of us was flat. My mother explained that we lived at the southernmost point a glacier had reached in the last ice age, that the glacier had come as far as our farm, then left everything there it had scraped off the continent on its way. So there were hills, valleys, and strange rock formations.

We had a pond that supported trout—a waterfall freshened it, and it was, to my child's eyes, a picture book perfect place. So beautiful it was—and my father added to that scenic place by taking up the twin country affectations of smoking a pipe and fly-fishing. He rarely caught anything. Even at the height of summer, the water was cold to the marrow of your bones, except for a shallow part near what my mother turned into a beach.

If my father caught a trout, he'd let me hold it a moment, once he'd removed the hook, and I could feel its muscles convulsing, willing itself back to the water, eyes shocked wide in the dull light of the air, the fish gasping but alive. My father told me that the soft, slippery coating that came off on my hands was the fish's immortality.

That part of the world was a place of fierce spring thunderstorms, often accompanied by tornadoes. I must have been eight the night a bolt of lightning swelled in the night sky and lit our whole farm like a miniature version of itself inside a snow globe; the lightning couldn't have struck more than a quarter-mile from my bedroom window where I crouched, my chin level with the sill, watching for tornadoes with my older brother.

The next day a bloated mare lay in the field, her feet straight out. A night or two later, my parents burned the corpse and called their friends to come and see, though we were kept away.

My brother, three years older, holding my hand, led me out to the field to see the mare's skeleton. Under a heavy gray sky, the stench of burnt flesh made us hold our hands over our mouths and noses. Bits of flesh—white and brown patches of the mare's skin and coat —still clung to the bone. And nestled inside the skeleton of the mare, I saw—the tiny skeleton of a foal. That day Death told me what he could take away. Ashes drifted in the air like snowflakes.

I must have slept for hours, days. Todd tells me that he came right back. He'd just had to run back to the inn for his license—he'd taken it out of his wallet when we'd checked in, left it at the front desk—and felt sure I wouldn't miss him; he didn't think he was gone even ten minutes.

And yet I woke up the following day in a strange bed. I remember a daybed with an ocher coverlet. Later, in the room above the store, a bed and the weight of a homemade quilt, blissfully comforting. The feel of a spoon held to my lips, soup. A woman—not old, but her hair was white—held the spoon. Her eyes looked intently into mine, but she never spoke. Then I slept again.

I felt flush, hot, as if I wanted to disrobe, throw back anything that covered me. I can't say if it was a fever. It felt like daylight went on and off, on and off. As if someone were blowing out and relighting the kerosene lantern by my bedside over the course of minutes rather than full days.

And I learned some things, though how I couldn't tell you. It was as though someone—the white-haired woman?—was passing into me a story, but not in words. Something the women in the postcard might have said, or what I allowed myself to imagine. My dreams were reels of images from earlier times, of old kitchen tools, egg beaters, tarnished spoons, crockery, a bellows for raising a fire from the embers of the night before.

My bicycle shoes stood paired beside a wardrobe. A pair of slippers had been provided me by someone—ivory silk, seeming almost as from a bride's trousseau. I wore them, and they fit perfectly, and I moved around the room in the haze of dusk. It was as if I was awakening from dreaming, moving around in the gray early morning light, before cocks began to crow, hours before true dawn.

I was pregnant and felt life move inside me.

Todd would say to our friends, "She had this wild ride, to hear her tell it." My belly round, his hand on it. We sat next to each other after dinner on the sectional in our living room in our fine old house in a suburb west of Sacramento. This time Todd shaped the story for his college roommate, Best man Ben, and Ben's girlfriend du jour. I forget her name, Margie, Maggie, or even Madeleine.

"To hear her tell it, I abandoned her up there on the mountain."

"He did! He was abandoning me up there. He decided I should join a cult. He thought it would be good for the baby, no doubt. Lots of mothers around. A strong father figure?" I smiled and looked his way, playing my part, as if this were the revenge he had decided to exact, his way of humiliating me and my whole sex. I went along. I hadn't really seen the emotional math; I didn't know where this would end. Maybe I was past caring.

He still didn't know the baby was Peter's; it had to be. Somehow my intended confession became a sharp knife I kept hidden in a drawer, one I slipped from its sheath from time to time to admire, noting how the light gleamed on the blade as I turned it gently one way and then the other in my hand.

"Fresh mountain air," he went on. "I get back. Pick her up. She says, 'Where have you been? It's been days!'"

I raised my hand, showing three fingers. "It was. Literally. Days."

He shook his head. "Ten minutes, and when I get there, she's wearing this… getup!" He always makes a dramatic pause at this point in the story, as if he's telling it for the first time. "Anyway, there she is like she'd been playing dress-up—some kind of kimono or something, these silk slippers that looked like they ought to be in a museum, her hair all over the place like the Bride of Frankenstein—"

Margie (if that was her name) interrupted, making a spiral gesture with an extended forefinger beside her temple, her small wrist turning in circles. "She wore hers up, more of a beehive. Black. Gray lightning bolts." She draws the lightning bolts running up her imaginary Bride of Frankenstein's hair.

I laughed for real. She wouldn't stay with that lacrosse-coach bozo who brought her to dinner and manhandled her under the mistletoe. (Yes, it was the holidays!) Todd's jaw stiffened, then he continued, his voice soft as if talking to someone mentally deficient, not just me—both of us. Two dumb cows, man-hating women.

Even speaking softly, he said it with a coarseness—gravel in his voice—not even pretending he wasn't angry. "Honey. Go put it on. Show our guests."

I uncrossed my legs. Recrossed them. I made a grudging performance of removing Todd's hand from my belly, stood, and went upstairs. I could hear him, even as I got changed in our bedroom, the door open, his voice echoing off the plaster. For a moment, I closed my eyes and bathed in the gold-green light of the store.

"Anyway, you can see how all this looks. I get her in the truck. I throw some money at the old guy behind the counter—for the clothes—and we drive all the way home. I don't really know what to say. I'm kind of in shock. It didn't seem at all funny at the time."

"It wasn't funny," I said as I came down the stairs, mock pouting. "And it's not true we didn't talk. Remember?" I paused, stroked my belly—six months along. I made my voice tiny to please him. "I asked you, 'Did you get my bicycle shoes?'"

Margie turns to me. "How far are you along?" But her face asks, Why do you let him do this to you? And she was right. What had been coming a long time had finally arrived. I had to make my break with this bleak life, this marriage.

On New Year's Eve, the snow was heavy, blinding, unseasonal, and you in my belly pressed against the wheel as I drove. I welcomed the thick silence that fell over the mountains, a silence apart from the noise of the SUV.

I kept the 4Runner on the road by the occasional wink of a yellow reflector on a guardrail or sign, by some kind of prayer, though I've never been the praying kind. The minutes were hours long. I grew low on gas and feared the sound of the engine guttering out in the blizzard but saw nowhere to buy fuel.

I weighed turning around and going back. I finally slowed, pulled over, stopped, and—lowering my face to the backs of my hands on the wheel—I cried, sobbing out all the sorrow and anger in me.

Eventually, I looked up. I sensed a dim green light just slightly bleeding into the darkness inside the vehicle, and I looked around. In a moment, when the blizzard relented, I saw an ice locker on a porch. A kerosene lantern in an upstairs window. I had somehow pulled over in drifting snow across the road from the store in Clear Lake, the landscape transfigured by winter. Wrong in my belief that I had miles to go.

Chuck, the shopkeeper—in the same plaid shirt or another like it

—helped me into the store and sat me in the chair by the stove. He smiled. I looked around to see if the woman with the white hair appeared, and the girl. They had not.

The man brought me water in a paper cup printed with the image of an endless, eternal vine. I drank the water, and I felt the goodness fill me. In the compact old mining town nearby, there were three churches, not one of them flanked by a cemetery. Why? Where did the departed go?

But ah, you, my child, daughter of Peter, thrive. The others, those mortals we once knew, exhaust themselves, mere swift shadows in our days and years. Figures ripple in the wavy glass at the front of the store and find the door locked. They press their hands against the glass and bring their faces close to try to see in. We watch, hidden in the dark, their eyes blind to our light. We are home, and they are not. I have white hair, and you, my child, are the girl of my visions.

LAST RESORT

A week at the Iberostar Grand Hotel at Punta Cana in the Dominican Republic was not unfamiliar to us. We had gone to that resort eight times already, but not for several years since the Covid-19 pandemic stopped us from traveling there or anywhere else. And travel was something Terry and I loved to do: road trips, cruises, and airplanes to resorts worldwide. After meeting over twenty years ago, we started traveling and never stopped until Covid. We like all travel, especially if it's done first class, and this trip to the Iberostar Grand in Punta Cana has all the luxurious features of our other trips and is also nothing like anything we've ever done.

This time we take a limo service to the airport to be fancy and avoid the park-and-shlep. Even before Terry had Alzheimer's, our combined lack of direction added twenty minutes to all transportation transitions. We have a restaurant meal before our 6 a.m. departure. I buy some mint candy and a small tube of hand cream; Terry buys some M&M candy. We share gum. And we also share a large bottle of water.

On the plane, we enjoy the settling in, the flight attendants' attention, who already like us because Terry is mindful of them as people and calls them by their names instead of the usual "Miss" or "Stewardess." She expresses appreciation to every single COPA Airline representative who speaks to her. We seem like people who will not be screaming for more booze or more peanuts. And we know we will like being up front: no one loves business class more than people who routinely flew coach for many years.

We are smiling from the moment we board. I get to sit near the window this time. That was Terry's place at one time, but she doesn't like window seats now. "Too many things I don't know," is her explanation. It's evident that we like each other and are happy to be traveling together. As soon as we get our beverages (in glasses!), we toast to having a delightful trip. Terry adds, "And to the Vargas Clinic." I take a more petite swallow of my champagne.

The Vargas Clinic is in Santa Domingo, where we will go after staying at the Grand Hotel. It is a nonprofit organization offering accompanied suicide. For the past twenty-plus years, the Vargas Clinic has been the only place to go if you are an American citizen who wants to die and if you are not certifiably terminally ill with no more than six months to live. This is the current standard in the United States. Even in the nine right-to-die states, about which many older or chronically ill Americans harbor end-of-life fantasies and which I researched, at Terry's direction, until we discovered that the only place in the world for painless, peaceful, and legal suicide is the Vargas Clinic, in the suburbs of Santa Domingo.

After Terry's diagnosis and before our trip to the Vargas Clinic, I looked to find whatever I thought would give her pleasure. I turn to our local casino to brighten our days because Terry has been happy and, I believe, a competent blackjack player since I've known her. I don't know anything about gambling; I know that I think it's idiotic. Sports betting, slot machines, Keno, Texas Hold 'em, baccarat, and blackjack—it seems a lot like throwing money out the window, but that's because I do not get the thrill of the chase. Terry does.

I noodle around the Iberostar website and read this:

Casino now open at the Iberostar Grand Hotel Bávaro!

Spend an evening in the elegant new casino at Iberostar Grand Hotel

Bavaro de Punta Cana, designed to provide an exciting experience that makes a night of fun gaming. The stunning casino has a variety of slot machines and table games with a range of denominations, so regardless of your level of interest or experience, there is something for every guest. Located next to the lobby, bring your friends to play a few games, then head to the exquisite Lobby Bar and relax over an artfully-prepared cocktail. After an evening of world-class gourmet dining, stop by to try your luck! Approach our casino hosts for weekly prizes and giveaways!

That will thrill Terry. When we previously stayed at the Iberostar Grand Hotel, we had headed over to the Hard Rock Resort for gambling at their casino; now, we won't have to.

"You could play blackjack at the Iberostar now," I say. I don't know if she can still play blackjack. She played online until a few months ago but stopped because she couldn't keep the count any longer, even with jotting it down. Maybe playing in person will be different.

"Do you want to see a picture of our room?" I say. They've redone all the rooms since our last stay.

"I would…" Then, "I don't remember what they were like then," she replies.

I show her a picture. It's just about the same as before, with maybe different colors and prints on the walls, a bland version of grand, with tufted carpeting and a polyester bedspread, and it's now $1,100 a night. We will be spending money we don't have. While we kept expenses down for ourselves, we had to loan money to all our kids to keep them afloat during the pandemic. That took most of our savings. And the Vargas Clinic got the rest.

The reason things are financially strained is because I was suddenly retired, three years ahead of schedule—the pandemic again, and Terry had to quit work almost two years ago when she could no longer do her job. But still, we made do. She could gamble a little, and we got decent meals brought to us by Grubhub and other meal services.

Terry wanted to go down to the casino as soon as we got to our room. I agreed, and we headed there without even changing from our travel clothes. I take a book with me since she leaves me alone for hours. I'll sit in some plushy chair off the reception area with low lighting and scented air while she goes play blackjack. I'll order at least two Piña Coladas while she has a Mai Tai, only one while gambling. After that, she'll order a club soda with many slices of lime.

I'll read and people-watch while she wins and loses, and maybe wins $500, after a couple of hours. I want her face to light up, as it used to over so many things: let's get two pizzas instead of one, both kinds of cheesecake, go to Paris for a month when we retire, build a grape arbor—hell, open a winery! Drive to Las Vegas, stay up all night and remain in bed all morning; watch The Lady Vanishes twice in a row, and Casablanca three times—that's what I miss. Spontaneous delights all!

What is hard now is doing things with her, and she stops, forgets where she is or who she's with.

Once so easy and pleasant, living with Terry has become unpleasant, if not complicated, and demanding in many ways. She's doesn't engage with me in banter as she once did. I miss that. She was once so witty and quick with her retorts on almost any subject. And she was competitive with me. No, it wasn't the usual marital game of who-gets-what/fair-is-fair. Instead, it was finding ways to best the other and then get a reward that each enjoyed.

Terry's not performing the way she used to in the casino. She lacks interest, mainly, in winning or losing, and is mostly losing now. Once, she only spent an hour or two a day on the tables; recently, it's been at least three or four. And I miss her when she's doing something that has nothing to do with me.

I see that she's not enjoying herself. The casino doesn't appeal; the idea of gambling, the wish to win or chase, has faded. Practicing blackjack hours on her laptop, as she used to, getting ready for an evening of cards with a dealer and other players seemed a lifetime ago. Terry never brings up the idea of a gambling holiday again.

◆ ◆ ◆

All fall I was making suggestions for trips to take: Florence and Paris, or one or the other, they could be lovely in late November, I say (which is not what I think; I think it will beyond melancholy and I will regret that I don't drink heavily).

I remind her of the extended cruises we went on twice; each time one of my parents died. She loved it, and I reminded her of all the things she loved about it: the suite we booked, the exclusive dining areas we got to go to. And the private beaches we got dropped off on and frolicked about for a few hours, naked and too old to be naked and still happy about it, like extras in a Fellini movie. The big afternoon tea that allowed us to skip lunch, where she could drink two pots of Earl Grey, eat dozens of tiny sandwiches, and stuff herself with blueberry scones.

I remind her of the evening when we walked to the buffet in formal wear and had a second dinner, much bigger than the first. And the flirtatious masseuse, who managed to make both of us feel irresistible. She smiles distantly at all of this. And then, I go online to show her some photos of her very favorite hotel in San Francisco. I talk about the morning we had breakfast in the room, took a walk, and came back for another, fancier breakfast, and she shakes her head, the way you do when someone has insisted on reminding you of unimportant detail.

One day, after breakfast, Terry says, "I should get birdseed. We don't have any. I put birdseed out all year round, and then a few weeks ago, there were bugs in the seed, so I stopped for a couple of weeks."

"You stopped for a year," I say, and I think, What in Jesus's name is wrong with you? Who cares?

Obviously, I do, because I wish to make the point that the birds have suffered and that even though the bug-in-the-seed problem was terrible (and it was gross: winged bugs flew out like in a horror movie), she didn't deal with it for almost two years, in fact. I am, apparently, committed to telling her it was more than two weeks. Terry's in charge of all things avian, and I've affronted her by telling her that she hasn't cared for the birds.

I try hard not to say things like this, but every once in a while, my need to prove a point, such a base and unattractive need, rises, and I meet it by telling her things that she doesn't need to hear. I'm ashamed of myself, but then Terry turns on me and says she can't understand why she is being grilled about birdseed. She gets a little loud and very irritable, and she leaves abruptly, and I'm glad, not only because she's gone but since she yelled at me, quite unfairly (you could say that I was pressing the point about the unfed birds, but I wasn't grilling her); I don't feel ashamed anymore.

Days later, we are still talking about birdseed, after a fashion. Terry sees the birds outside the window while we're having breakfast and says, "I should get some birdseed." I nod only.

We go to couples therapy. It looks like couples therapy since we are sitting next to each other, facing a counselor, in a small room with beige carpeting, and we look at each other at intervals, fondly and nervously. A couple of times, my eyes welled up with tears. It's not like couples therapy because neither of us hopes that the other will change. Whoever Terry is now is who he's going to be, for as long as our life together lasts. Then I think, well, that's true of most couples therapy.

In couples therapy, months after the diagnosis but before the acceptance from the Vargas Clinic, Terry says, "I think I'd like to go on one last vacation before I die."

Donna was our counselor, and she'd been leading Terry toward discussing ways she can enjoy life again, said, "Ah. A vacation. That's a fine idea."

Me (inside): Are you fucking kidding me? Arrange a trip? Now? And where? Someplace we've been and loved, which will now be some half-baked, propped-up version of the real thing? Some new place that I will help you negotiate while you chafe at my attention and wander off in some foreign city, prey to anyone that sees opportunity in your bewildered look?

Me: Oh. A vacation. Sure. Yes.

By the time we get home, I hope that Terry will have forgotten the big vacation. I ask her if maybe she wants a little holiday. I don't mention a big holiday. A week ago, my sister Carol said Terry might like one last big girlfriend's shopping trip to Palm Springs and that I could, after all, stay nearby in a motel while Terry, she, and two other girlfriends shop for hours and then finish up with long chatty dinners afterward. "She always liked those trips," Carol says.

I know that Terry enjoyed those outings and that Carol and she always got along well on them, buying things at two outlet malls and not at the high-end stores on El Paseo. Carol knows something about shopping since she was a buyer at May Company before going bankrupt. She made calls to friends to see who else would like to go with them but had no takers. "No one wants to go because of what happened last time," she says. "Not even those who didn't go last time."

I understand the reluctance on their part. Yet Terry has been her happiest going off with her girlfriends on shopping trips, and I want her to experience that again. "All happiness is fleeting," I remember reading somewhere, but I see now that there is fleeting. Then there is the actual and wall-like impossibility of ever experiencing this kind of happiness again, even once, even next week, let alone a year from now. Doors are closing around us all the time. I reluctantly and hopefully call Carol and tell her to keep calling others. Even if just one or two of her friends want to go, they should do it. "That's what friends are for" is another line that comes to mind. If not this, what else can they do for her?

And her doctors have failed her, including her internist, Good Time Charlie, the doctor who hates bad news. When Terry came to him a few years earlier, in 2018, complaining about her memory, GTC was all reassurance, and Terry came home and told me so.

When we went to him for our B12 discussion, Good Time Charlie was, as always, pleased to see Terry and didn't say anything about seeing me. He looked at the referral from the neurologist and said, "So, vitamin B12. It used to be given by injection. That injection had been the gold standard, but–good news—not anymore. It should be taken in a massive dose, sublingually —dissolving under the tongue, and she should take it for the rest of her life." Charlie explains that he's ordering a second, superior B12 test that will reveal, he hopes, another possible cause of the B12 deficiency, atrophic gastritis, in which the stomach lining has thinned, and absorption is a problem. He looks at us pleasantly and half rises out of his seat. I see that we are dismissed, and I see that Terry has no wish for further discussion.

Terry's blood test comes back normal, and I'm glad, and I'm still angry and puzzled about the last meeting and left a voice mail for Charlie.

He calls me a few days later, and I tell him that I can't understand why he never asked about the referral from the neurologist or Terry's cognitive issues in the course of our meeting. He stammers and says that he assumed the referral was for headaches.

WHAT HEADACHES? I tell Charlie that if he looks at Terry's chart, he will see that Terry has barely ever had a headache in her life.

Charlie says, "OK," like a fourteen-year-old boy, mulish and nervous.

"What does that mean? Does this seem OK to you? OK, that you had no interest in why a neurologist referred a longtime patient? What's OK about that?"

"OK," he says.

"It is not OK," I say.

The good days still have sweetness. If I can't fall asleep quickly, I ask Terry if I can spoon her. She turns on her left side and nuzzles into me, closing the gap quickly to show that she wanted that too. And sometimes, like the old days (three years ago), I slide my hand through the button area of her nightgown and feel her amazingly smooth skin and smell the scent of her hair, which hasn't changed: John Masters Organics Shampoo for Normal Hair With Lavender and Rosemary.

We lie in bed and watch old movies such as Murder, She Said, written by Agatha Christie and starring Margaret Rutherford as Miss Marple; Terry on my shoulder and watching for no more than twenty minutes before she falls asleep. When she wakes up, she asks me to explain what went on after she dozed off, what the rocking chair was about or why the tennis ball was covered in blood. We eat some cookies and ice cream in bed, and I point out that there's been a change (not a bad thing, but still…) in the weather girl's outfits that tend to be more revealing of late. After we finish off the cookies, we brush the cookie crumbs onto the floor because no one is watching. I plump my pillow so vigorously it knocks everything off my nightstand, and she laughs and says that I'm a danger to myself and others. Those moments are all I want. I want a life filled with them. She sighs, and I sigh.

The bad days are pretty much the birdseed moment, all day long. Sometimes it's worse than the bickering over facts or the heavy gloom that descends on her, for which I do not blame her at all, but it makes for a dark house. Terry gets an email from an old classmate, asking if she'll be available for a class reunion next year. He's planning ahead and wants to get volunteers and a headcount. She writes a reply and then deletes it. Then a second, and deletes it as well. She wants to attend, but will it be possible?

Terry muses out loud about the class reunion for about ten minutes and says, with some sadness, "I'll have to decline. I don't know if I should give the reason." I agree. There's no denying present reality or her future. Saying "Yes, I can help, and count me in for attending" would be wrong, even if she wanted to with all her heart.

All fall, I veer between worrying about her and grim determination. A birthday party for a grandchild comes and goes, likewise that of an aunt, alike a dinner party at which Terry unexpectedly excels at a table game of Name That Quote, and I feel a fool to have worried at all; likewise, our family's own Oktoberfest, in which my son and eldest granddaughter, our number one, Isadora (we were with her the day she was born, a bit too soon, in the middle of a fix-up-the-new-house visit and we walked the halls and fielded calls and hugged and kissed everyone, including the nurses, did the atheists' version of prayer, and now Terry calls her Darling, to be on the safe side) come down from Seattle, my daughter and my daughter-in-law and our shining light, little Zora, come up from San Diego. We all go through a corn maze, with clues, and they get their faces or pumpkins painted, and there is a donkey ride, after which we all eat an enormous lunch at The Cheesecake Factory.

I have a memory of Zora waving from a small train that goes through a field and Izzy and the twins jumping from bale to bale in a hay tower. I cannot hold Terry in the picture. I know she went through the maze. I know she must have gone grinning down the big slide (there was never a big slide she didn't go down). I know she must have ordered the grilled corn and the fancy fries, but I cannot see her in my mind's eye.

I cannot see much of that fall, only pieces of Thanksgiving, Christmas, and New Year's. I know we celebrated them all, and I know she was there, and I know, for that matter, that I was there too, thinking, on the one hand, this will probably be the last and fearing that it would not be, that I will fail to help her, fail to help her get to The Vargas Clinic, to the other side of that stay at the Iberostar Grand Hotel stay, however, we must go. I remember Christmas because it is smaller than usual, just us and the kids and grandchildren, and I beg off having my sister and her family, and I hardly care that I am disappointing them all. I remember it only because there are photos of Terry and me, her grand in her mother's jewel-toned silk robe, me frowning, in my ragged robe. Sunlight is coming through the big window behind us, and I look like an old man on a long train ride, barely sitting up.

My sister had cried with me since the second appointment with the neurologist, when it took the doctor less than an hour to give Terry a mental-status exam and inform us that Terry almost certainly had Alzheimer's and had probably had it for several years, judging by her high IQ, her struggles with balance and proprioception, and her poor performance on the exam. It took Terry less than a week to decide that the "long goodbye" of Alzheimer's was not for her and less than a week for me to find The Vegas Clinic, at the end of several long Google paths.

From summer to winter, my sister Ellen, who loves me and loved Terry, did her best not to make suggestions, not to offer if-onlys, not to say that maybe Terry's Alzheimer's wouldn't be too bad or would progress very slowly, not to cry when I wasn't crying and not to pour out her own grief at the loss of one of her favorite people and our compatible foursome. (When they met for the first time, Twenty-two years ago, Terry went into Ellen's kitchen with her winning ways and said, "I really love your brother." My sister didn't turn around. She said, "He called you the love of his life. Hurt him, and I will kill you.")

Ellen called me early one morning in December when we were pretty sure that we'd cleared the hurdles for The Vargas Clinic and said, "Just tell me what you need." I said, "Reluctantly, I need some money. It costs twenty thousand, and I don't have it all." My big sister said, "I'll send you a check for thirty." We ended up spending every penny of it, between a couple of last big trips for Terry, she not working, my not working, our eating out all the time, sometimes lunch and dinner, at the nicest restaurants in town. We spend it on what was to be our last joint birthday celebration in Hollywood and on the week at the Iberostar Grand, and the limo services and the gaming tables and my sister Ellen flying in to keep me company on the flight home, on whatever makes bad months bearable, plus the cost of The Vegas Clinic itself (around $10,000 all-in).

On our last night at the resort, Terry and I toast each other, and we say, Here's to you, a little hesitantly, instead of what we usually say, Cent'anni (May we have a hundred years, a very Italian toast). There is no cent'anni for us; we won't make it to our next wedding anniversary.

We lean close to each other, kiss, and then we pull back, wondering what to say or do next. Both of us are aware we are doing all this for the last time.

We have to pack before going to bed. Or at least I do. She decided everything she brought would stay here, given away to the staff. How to explain that? She didn't want to tell anyone about her situation or her visit to the Vargas Clinic. Although, everyone had already learned that something was wrong with her and that this visit would probably be her last.

It was supposed to be nearly the same, like all the other past trips we'd taken there. If it all seemed normal initially, it didn't remain that way soon after arriving. I left her and went to the front desk area to check-in. I hadn't turned my attention away from her for more than a minute, but when I turned to check on her, she had disappeared. I found her soon enough at the curb front, anxious and frightened, not knowing where she was.

It was different this time being with her, to be together, but not with her. We had been at the resort three years before, only three years ago when I didn't have to hold my breath every time I turned my attention away from her, worrying that she might go off somewhere in a state of panic and be lost to me forever. And then I realized that soon, very soon, she would be lost to me forever.

COMEUPPANCE, OR
WHAT GOES AROUND
COMES AROUND

Brenda came believing I would help her. I was her brother, after all. Perhaps things between us weren't the best. Even so, she could count on me to give her a little money until she found a job or somehow got more money. Or, if I wouldn't give her money, I could give her and her children a place to stay for a while. I could guide her to someone at social services or lawyers and counselors—people who could help a person like her. I could play with her children, cook breakfast, buy lunch, let them use my washer and dryer and towels… be a brother to her in her time of need.

She came unannounced on a rainy Friday evening after I had finished my take-out Chinese food and pulled another beer from the fridge before my game began, Dodgers v. Giant, something I'd looked forward to seeing that night. No girlfriend, I'd broken up with Alice weeks ago and wanted to give myself some time to clear my head from that experience before I started dating again. I was twenty-seven years old, single, in decent shape, a college graduate with the unusual job of selling snap metal to foundries worldwide. I lived alone with my dog in a condo I'd purchased five years earlier.

That Friday, as she came down the road in the rain, Brenda was thirty-three and drove an old blue Escort our dad had bought her when she graduated from high school. She could now add a shattered windshield to the car's long list of ailments. She could barely see the road in front of her in the rain. Finally, she rolled down her window and leaned her head out to see.

The rain hit in her face and blew into the car, onto her two young boys, strapped into their car seats in back: Nick, who was three and a half, could sleep through anything, and Johnny, who would be eighteen months on Sunday, sat behind her, getting the worst of it and crying.

She'd left her husband, Billy—their father, as she'd call him now —an hour before, after he'd left her out of his sight for a minute. He said he was going down to Casey's to get himself a pack of cigarettes. He was going to walk. There was no sense in driving four blocks when he could save the gas and get a little fresh air. She told him to pick up a bag of hamburger buns, a big can of pork-n-beans, and some ketchup. A liter of Pepsi, too, if he could carry it all.

He looked back at her without suspecting a thing, saying nothing but, "Fine, will do." When she asked him to get a half-gallon of milk too, he looked back and snarled, "Holy fuck, Brenda, was there anything else?" By the time she saw him coming up the street again, the groceries she'd ordered swinging in plastic bags from his big keg-hauling arms, she was backing out the driveway. And when he came running toward the car, she just locked the doors and kept backing. He chased her into the street, took one of the bags and slammed it onto the hood, and with the other hit the windshield, smashing it. That was all he could do. She had their only car, and he'd never catch her on foot.

When the doorbell rang, my dog, Jonah, let out a bark. The two noises startled me. I tossed the remote onto the sofa, wondering who could be at my door in weather like this.

The bell rang again—DING DING DING!

I wondered who was out there, in this monsoon, ringing my bell at seven o'clock on a Friday?

I heard a toddler's voice outside: "Doggie! Mommy, listen—a doggie! Uncle Peter's got a doggie!"

Reluctantly, I stared into the peephole.

"Yes, Nick," Brenda said, her hand zooming large as she reached forward and pounded on the door. "Mommy heard you the first time."

I stepped back, squeezing the bridge of my nose. Should I pretend that I'm not home? I thought about it, but, in the end, I couldn't just let them stand in the rain.

"Come on! Come inside!" I held Jonah with one hand and the screen door open with the other. Brenda and her boys looked like someone had stood them in a shower stall and turned on the water. "Jesus Christ, how long were you out there?"

"Long enough," Brenda answered, hiking Johnny up on her hip, pulling Nick by the arm so he wouldn't go chasing after the dog. I closed the door behind them, and it didn't take long for her to tell me why she was here.

"I left him," she said breathlessly as if she'd just run up a flight of stairs.

It was hard to look at her. She looked terrible. She'd dyed her hair a cheap nectarine blond, and even with it soaking wet, dark roots showed from her scalp. Her face had hardened into something coarse and desperate in the months since I'd seen her... Or has it been longer? Yes, over a year now and approaching two. And while I knew it was dangerous to pity her, it was heartbreaking to look at her. What had happened to my older sister, who'd been such a pretty girl growing up?

"Jesus, you look like shit," she said. "How long have you been up?"

"Two days." I had just come off a double shift. I smiled at the boys, and for a moment, Johnny stopped crying.

"Did you hear what I said?" she asked.

She meant the part about leaving Billy. "Yes," I muttered, "I heard you."

"You don't seem very pleased."

Why had she thought I'd be pleased? "What made you decide to come here?"

She turned up her eyes and scoffed. "I seem to remember someone telling me I couldn't go to Mom and Dad's."

"Yeah, well, I didn't tell you to come here."

Her chin began to tremble, and hate welled in her eyes. She was holding Nick so tightly by the arm he was wincing. "Fine. We'll leave," she said, turning toward the door.

Johnny was crying again, and I covered the doorknob with my hand. "Spare me the histrionics, Brenda."

"Like I need this shit from you right now," she said, trying to pull my hand from the knob.

"I gave you the number to a shelter," I reminded her, not budging. "A place where he wouldn't be able to find you—"

"I'm not taking them to a shelter!" she shouted. "You can throw us out if you want, but I'm not taking them to some fucking shelter. No way."

I still had hold of Jonah's collar. The boys looked at me as though I might snap the dog's neck. "You're too good for that, are you?" I finally said. "A shelter's not swank enough for you?"

"Fuck you!" she shot back. "You just don't want us around. Admit it!"

Fair enough, I thought. "So why'd you come here, then?"

"I just told you."

I closed my eyes for a second, then lowered my voice. "You marry into poor white trash to show Dad that he can't control you, and then, when it isn't any fun anymore, when you've got the poor slob you married controlling you instead, you say enough of this bullshit and bolt, figuring you'll always have me to lean on, and Dad and Mom too, to pick up the tab, like they always have, until they're finally at peace in their graves—"

"Shut your mouth! Shut your fucking mouth!"

"It's always been that way, Brenda. Life everlasting, amen. So what do you want now? Tell me. Before Billy gets here."

"Go fuck yourself!"

"When's he going to get here?" I persisted.

"He doesn't even know where you live," she shot back, wiping her eyes with her sweatshirt. "I've got the car. I don't know how he'd get here."

Maybe it was true, and perhaps it wasn't, I thought, feeling ashamed, suddenly—such a display of profanity in front of such young eyes. "Let me get you some towels," I said.

"Thanks," she said as if it were about time.

I headed upstairs, Jonah following me. I knew what she was thinking now. No matter what she did, in my eyes, in Mom and Dad's, it was always the wrong thing. She'd finally gotten up the courage to leave Billy, which we'd been begging her to do for years, and instead of helping her, I wanted to send her away.

I grabbed towels from the linen closet, then felt in my back pocket to make sure my wallet was there, and I hadn't left it on the counter for her to go through. I went down and held out the towels, but her hands were full. I'd have to take one of the boys.

"I think you'll find Johnny less of a handful," she said.

That was hard to believe how he was crying, but I took him from her anyway. "You shouldn't be carrying them around like you do all the time," I said. "You're going to hurt your back again and end up in the hospital."

"I know. You don't need to tell me." She started drying herself and Nick, and when Johnny reached out for her and started to cry, she told him to be patient.

The thing was, it could be pleasant between Brenda and me from time to time. But the pleasant moments only made me wary of what was to come. One night, four years earlier, when she was living with me, Brenda said she'd make lasagna if I went to the store. We talked about what cheeses I'd buy—Fontina, I thought, instead of mozzarella, Romano instead of Parmesan—and while we were talking, I got a call from my girlfriend, who said three checks were missing from her checkbook. One had already come back, forged, for two hundred in cash.

After hanging up, I found one of the other checks, still blank, in with Brenda's things. I showed it to her, and she looked at me like it was no big deal and said she'd pay my girlfriend back. I told her to get out. I'd warned her before when something similar happened. She looked at me, stunned, wondering where she was supposed to go, and I told her I didn't care. She should have thought of that, maybe. She said something to provoke me even more, and I called her a crazy fucking bitch. She came at me as she had with Dad once before she came to live with me, and I smacked her back after she smacked me, and told her again what a bitch she was, and told her to leave—all within ten minutes of a discussion on what we would make for dinner.

Nick reached out for the dog, and Brenda pulled him back.

"I wanna play with the doggie!"

"Nick, will you give me a break, for God's sake?"

"No!"

"Let him pet the dog if he wants," I said, tired of seeing her wince in pain every time he hung from her arm. Christ, she'd had four back surgeries already, and she wasn't even forty. I moved to the kitchen, bouncing Johnny in my arms to keep him from crying. I took Nick by the hand now and turned to Jonah, who was crouched nervously by the refrigerator. "It's OK. He just wants to pet you."

"I'm sorry," I heard Brenda say from the hallway. "I should have called ahead. But I don't have your new number, and Mom and Dad, every time I ask them for it, just make up some story."

Of course, she knew why. After stealing from my girlfriend and floating hot checks all over town, and after my phone wouldn't stop ringing from all the people looking for her, I changed my number to an unlisted one. I asked Mom and Dad not to give it to her.

"Well, I can imagine it's not easy," I said, squatting beside Jonah, guiding Nick's hand along Jonah's neck. "Calling ahead when your phone's disconnected."

"Billy didn't pay the bill."

"That's it," I said, ignoring her and letting Johnny pet the dog. "Lightly, though. Real soft. No, no, don't pull his fur. He doesn't like his fur pulled."

The boys had grown since the last picture I'd seen of them: Nick with his mom's indigo eyes, giggling at the antics of the photographer, hugging Johnny, whose smile seemed reluctant. Mom had given me the picture during one of my visits home. "Brenda sent us two," she'd said. "She asked me to give you one. So take it along. They're your nephews, after all."

I took the picture home and had it framed. I kept it on my dresser.

The boys petted Jonah, who sat panting, looking proud. Nick reached out and grabbed his tongue. "No, no, no—" I took his hand.

"Let his tongue alone. Would you like it if I grabbed your tongue?" Jonah, seeing his opportunity, took off for the living room.

"You can let Nick go," said Brenda. "I'll catch him."

I let go of Nick's hand, and he ran past her. She started into the living room after him, but I told her to stop, to let him go. I put Johnny down. "Let them go nuts," I said.

I could see a kind of victory in Brenda's eyes. I was going to let them stay.

"What about clothes for them?" I asked after a minute. "Shouldn't they get into some dry clothes?"

"In the car," Brenda answered. "I was just waiting to see if you were home."

I stared out at Jonah, running around the coffee table, the boys chasing him and screaming.

"So, should I get them?" Brenda said. "The clothes?"

I pretended not to hear. "So, how long do you think it'll take?" I asked. "How long before he comes to my door, looking for you?"

She didn't know what to say. She didn't want to ruin things now that they seemed all right again. "I told you, he doesn't have a car."

"Well, surely someone he knows does, or he'll get a ride, or a taxi, whatever," I replied. "Not having a car won't keep him from getting here."

She said that even if he could get one, he still didn't know where I lived.

I would find out later that that wasn't exactly true. She'd shown him my place once when he'd taken her to the university for her first back surgery. She was hoping he'd forgotten or that he'd get lost and give up and go home.

Jonah was getting tired of being chased, so I grabbed the remote from the counter and flipped through the channels until I found an old episode of "Mister Ed."

"Go out and get what you need for the night," I said. "I'll keep an eye on the boys."

"Thank you," she replied, in that pitiful tone of hers, like I was hiding her from the Nazis.

"I'll order a pizza," I said to the sink. "You can take a shower, give the boys a bath if you want," I added, laughing—gleeful—wondering how generous I could become if I dug deep and put out some effort. "I've got more towels—shampoo, conditioner, dry socks—everything you could possibly want!"

Brenda went out to the car, and the boys were content in front of the television, listening to the talking horse. It was a good time to run up to my room and ensure there wasn't anything for Brenda to steal. While I was at it, I'd change the sheets for her. The boys could sleep in the spare room, on the futon, and I'd try to get some sleep on the sofa down here, with Jonah, close to the door, in case anyone called.

Tomorrow she and the boys would be gone, one way or the other. To her parents? Unlikely... Too many burned bridges. With girlfriends? Even less likely. If she had any left, none wouldn't be supportive at this point. In the end, she and the boys will end up in a shelter. At least there, they wouldn't have a history with her. Was this Karma? Absolutely, and I felt good about it.

I slept well that night, probably the best night's rest I'd had since, well, never. It was that good. Since we were children, my sister had been a thorn in my side. She had finally had her comeuppance... what I said would happen to her after the first time I suffered for something she had done. What? I don't even recall now. All I remember is how it felt, how I cried, and how good it would feel when she got her comeuppance.

NOT MUTUALLY EXCLUSIVE

"That's not mutually exclusive," my dad was fond of saying. It was his way of explaining seemingly unexplainable things. Growing up, I must have heard him say that a thousand times or more. He was a simple man doing a simple job all his life, that of a locksmith, but he came from a complicated family and had a complicated family himself.

He met his father just once in his life because his father left his mother only weeks after he was born and saw him finally shortly before his father died while mountain climbing near Yosemite. His own family consisted of five children: two sets of twins, all girls, born to twins he married, Shiela and Shelly, and me, Alan. He married Shiela first, and she died during childbirth. Later, he married Shelly, and they had another set of twins, and after me, the lone boy in the family.

His explanation for all this? "That's not mutually exclusive."

He got a lot of mileage out of this observation, whether used as a non sequitur or an actual answer. As platitudes go, it's a pretty uncompromising one: it doesn't offer reassurance or optimism, and it certainly doesn't provide any certainty.

In using it, saying that two things can be true, my father pointed out that truths, like feelings, don't eclipse each other—they only complicate each other. For example, maybe someone hurt you even though he loves you, and perhaps this is something you will do yourself someday.

Mourning a beloved parent's long illness doesn't mean never resenting it. Likewise, resenting a parent's absence doesn't mean that the parent is not loved. Maybe abusive people are sometimes witty and creative people addicted; maybe charming people are sometimes sociopaths and deceptive people survivors; maybe people sometimes behave carelessly, even though they care. And perhaps we don't need to believe or remember or feel just one thing about any person or situation. Maybe, in fact, we shouldn't.

"That's not mutually exclusive,"

There is nothing sentimental or overly sanguine about any of this. "Both things can be true" doesn't demand that we look only at the positive, the negative, or that we try to make one thing the only relevant variable in our moral or emotional calculus. Instead, it demands that we allow all the variables to sit uneasily together in our minds and try to be open to the full range of nuance in our lives and relationships.

Again: "That's not mutually exclusive."

This credo is perhaps similar to Keats's notion of "negative capability"—the belief that good art must acknowledge the bottomless complexity of the world and the essential uncategorizability of the people in it. Both great art and great people seem unwilling to indulge in simple answers.

Once again: "That's not mutually exclusive."

On a personal note and more to the point at hand, bad memories do not erase good ones. I am here to say a few words at my father's funeral.

We can feel empathy at the same time as uncomprehending anger —maybe it's then, in fact, that we're actually feeling it the most. And maybe our task in life isn't to resolve these contradictions. Maybe our task is just to live with them.

My father left his family when I was sixteen without any explanation. Except, of course, his departing words, which were, you guessed it, "That's not mutually exclusive."

DREW AND THE FUTURE OF FOREIGN TRAVEL

Drew Weinstein stood plaintively in front of the administrative assistant's desk, Irene Craig, a huge woman perched on a chair with wheels. The edge of her broad desk was lined with purportedly useful items: hand sanitizer, a bowl of cough drops, myriad trays for myriad forms—things that also offered another wall of protection against visitors with unreasonable requests. Weinstein helped himself to a dollop of hand sanitizer as the woman finished a phone call.

Weinstein was fit by middle-aged standards, with a shaved head and a neat gray goatee. He was wearing jeans and a polo shirt, the de facto uniform for male members of society these days since the trade wars made anything produced out of country prohibitively expensive.

"No, no, no," the administrative assistant told the caller. "A mistake like that on Form 2386A is entirely different. You would still have to pay—" She paused as the caller squeezed in some words. "All of that information is available online," she continued. She gave Drew Weinstein a look suggesting her profound annoyance that so many members of the public had not read the latest State Department issued advisories on international travel.

Weinstein looked at his watch. How long will this take, he thought. The administrative assistant told the anxious caller for a second time that the information they were seeking was available online. She hung up and peered at Drew Weinstein over the hand sanitizer and the bowl of cough drops. "Yes?"

"I need five minutes with the Regional Agent," Drew Weinstein said.

"Is this about a travel plan?" the administrative assistant asked.

"Yes," Weinstein said.

"All the forms are online."

"This is for a new state."

The woman's phone rang, prompting her to roll her chair to the side of the L-shaped desk. "International programs, please hold," she instructed and then rolled back to Weinstein. "They're all online," she said. "You fill out the New Travel Request Form based on your ultimate destination. We review them on a rotating basis."

"This is very time-sensitive," Weinstein said. He slid a sheet of paper between the candy bowl and three stacked metal trays.

"When would this be for?" the administrative assistant asked as she took the form.

"This month," Weinstein said. "We need to leave in three weeks." The woman laughed, shaking her head as if Drew Weinstein had just stated his attention to leap off the roof and fly. "I need to talk to your boss," Weinstein repeated. "This opportunity has come up very quickly."

The woman perused Weinstein's request form. "You can't go there that quickly," she said.

"Can you please get me five minutes with him?"

"To go here?" she asked, waving the form. "It's dangerous—chaotic. It's too new. You can't take tourists there. Is this serious?"

"We have an invitation," Weinstein said. The administrative assistant stared with disapproval through thick, round glasses at the form he had filled out. "There is no prohibition in any of your advisories," Weinstein continued.

"Well, of course, there isn't," the woman said. She was flustered that Drew had turned her favorite weapon against her. "The advisory on that region hasn't been updated since last spring, and this . . . well, this is all new."

"That's why I need to speak to the Regional Agent," Weinstein implored.

"He's not going to like this," she said.

Ben Gilbert, the Deputy Regional Agent for Travel, was free at two o'clock. Drew Weinstein grabbed the appointment, even though it conflicted with the beginning of his afternoon program. He sent an email to his assistant telling them to begin the scheduled talk without him. Drew Weinstein had warned the people signed up for the trip at every turn that their proposed travel was a long shot. They would have to bob and weave their way through the State Department bureaucracy, a system finely engineered to stall travel to certain parts of the world, rather than encourage it. And what they were planning was extraordinary. "That's crazy," Weinstein's wife had said when he received the invitation. "Really?"

Ben Gilbert was a compact man with a bushy head of gray hair and a matching mustache. His title suggested a swashbuckling adventurer who had visited the far corners of the earth. In fact, Ben Gilbert had been promoted to his position from the general counsel's office, where he had overseen risk mitigation for the travel programs abroad. "The only good travel is local travel," Ben was fond of saying. Over the years, he had directed more medical evacuations than he could remember. He had worked with the State Department to bring a student home who had run afoul of the Kuwaiti government. (There were rumors of a relationship with the daughter of a member of the royal family.) He had paid a "processing fee" to get two students out of a Togolese prison after they got drunk and vomited on a statue of the president. Ben Gilbert's best days were when his phone did not ring, especially in the middle of the night.

"Is this even legal?" Ben asked as he perused Drew Weinstein's memo for the meeting. "Why don't we wait for things to settle down?"

"We have an invitation from one of my colleagues at another location of our travel agency. She can arrange homestays for us—"

"Homestays?" Ben interrupted. "There's so much lingering animosity."

"We'll be guests," Weinstein said. "The healing process has to begin at some point."

"I'm not sure this is even an international program," Ben protested.

"According to the Treaty of Chicago, we'll be crossing a sovereign international border," Weinstein explained. "We need travel documents—"

"How do you get there?" Ben interrupted.

"Through Mexico City."

Ben played nervously with his mustache and then stared up at a large map of the world on his office wall. "We don't even have new maps yet," he said. "They've got that big meeting coming up with the final negotiations—the debt, the military, and the seat on the UN Security Council. This stuff is complicated."

Weinstein stifled a bitter laugh. "That's why I'm going," he said. "The people who signed on so far are excited."

"They don't know any better," Ben said. "The only good travel is local travel. I just spent four days getting a kid out of North Korea. He had a weekend free on the China program, and he thought it would be fun to go to Pyongyang."

"This is not North Korea," Weinstein said. "Representatives have been going back and forth for months. There's no more violence. It's all diplomacy now."

"Things could flare up again," Ben said.

Weinstein shrugged. "Isn't that true anywhere?"

Ben stared over Weinstein's head at a certificate on the wall recognizing five years of service as President of Risk Management Society of America. "I just brought back three young people who thought it would be a good idea to go samba dancing in a favela outside Rio. Do you know what a favela is?" he asked.

"I do," Weinstein said.

"They got robbed and beat up. They were lucky it wasn't worse."

"We will be guests living in people's homes. It's the opposite of wandering into a favela."

"Maybe," Ben said noncommittally. "I'd have to run it by the Regional Agent."

"My understanding is that you have the authority to approve any travel."

Ben Gilbert stared intently at Weinstein. "If you are going here," he said, holding up Weinstein's form and pausing dramatically, "he's going to have to sign off."

Drew Weinstein hustled across the town square to the squat brick building that was once a Hilton Hotel, but now American Express Travel, where his travel seminars were held. Weinstein climbed the steps quickly to the small room on the third floor, where about two dozen people were gathered around a square conference table with their laptops and notebooks and water bottles spread haphazardly in front of them.

Thirty-two people had initially been signed up for Weinstein's travel group. Six of them dropped out after the Separation. Three others dropped out for financial reasons, despite American Express's efforts to cushion the economic disruption. Certain additional fees and extras were reduced, deferred, or waived entirely. Weinstein was getting half salary, as were most of his colleagues. The goal, the President of American Express, stated in every speech and meeting was to keep the business operating until there was "a new political equilibrium."

There were signs of normalcy. "There are blueberries," Marjorie Fried told Weinstein as she passed him on the way out of the local food co-op that morning. These were the new metrics of daily life, even as the news headlines described the macro-chaos: wrangling over control of the navy's carrier groups; twenty-five thousand federal prisoners released early because of a dispute over who should pay the corrections officers; fewer than half of eligible seniors getting their Social Security checks. But there were blueberries on the shelves again. Prices had begun to stabilize too. More and more people were using the new currency. Still, when Weinstein took his car to have the snow tires put on, the business owner suggested payment in some form other than cash. Weinstein offered him an old cashmere sweater, which he had eagerly accepted.

Drew Weinstein climbed the stairs to the third floor. He could hear attendees talking as he approached the room. He walked in and tried to slide unobtrusively into a seat, but the discussion stopped. One of the attendees had written "Blame Canada?" on the whiteboard. Weinstein motioned for them to continue the conversation, but they were too eager for news. "Are we going?" one of them asked.

"They didn't say no," Weinstein said. "So it may still be a go." As an amateur travel historian, Weinstein wanted people to see unusual lands and places, to appreciate how different things may be in other parts of the world. And in this case, the big patterns, the relentless forces that had caused the Separation, rather than trying to drink from the headlines spewing at them like a firehose. They were all seeing the same news alerts: resignations of top military leaders; the temporary capital in Boston; rumors that Oregon and Washington would soon join California. Drew Weinstein had found the recent changes to be an instructive tool for probing the foundations of what was happening. "We should seek to travel to places where news is happening," he urged again.

A gangly senior citizen with long, unruly hair and one of the regulars on Weinstein travel groups, Jonathan Brooks, stood to speak for the Blame Canada team. "If the Ottawa government had not offered a defense and monetary union," he asserted, "the Separation would not have been possible. It's that simple." He read from an editorial that had appeared in the New York Times: "It was nothing but lots of hot air for pundits and blowhard politicians until the Canadians offered a place of refuge for the disgruntled New England states."

Weinstein stood and offered his opinion: "For as long as humans have tried to make sense of the world around them," he began in a dramatic tone, "they have imputed causality where none exists. The sun does not revolve around the earth, and Canada did not cause the Separation." Several attendees banged on the table in support, drawing a knowing nod from Weinstein. "The Separation began the moment a group of white men tried to build the foundation of a republic on the sands of slavery. Abraham Lincoln, great man though he was, merely staved off the inevitable."

"What about California and Texas?" someone else asked. "Both of those states broke away without any deal in place with Canada." He was originally from Boston and was in finance before he retired, and there were rumors that he had somehow made a great deal of money due to the Separation.

"It wouldn't have happened if New England hadn't gone first," Weinstein answered quickly. "And New England wouldn't have seceded without Canadian protection."

Brooks interjected, "You're still missing the point. Some version of this was inevitable. It's like . . ." he paused, searching for a metaphor. "It's like you've got a growing mound of oily rags piling up in the furnace room. Canada is just the guy who turned on the furnace. The real problem is two hundred and fifty years of oily rags."

"But if no one turns on the furnace, you have time to clean the oily rags up," Weinstein said. His background included parents who were immigrants from Russia. They had lived through the collapse of the Soviet Union. Weinstein often interjected that perspective into the discussions.

There was a rapping on the open door. A young girl with long flowing hair looked to Drew Weinstein. "Someone from the agency office for travel just called. They want to see you."

"Now?" Weinstein asked.

"Apparently," the young girl answered. "Are you the one heading the tour group trying to take that trip?" Weinstein nodded as he processed the summons. "Then that means you." the girl said.

"Keep going," Weinstein told the group. "I like how you've moved the conversation on this topic."

"Without Canada's assurances of protection, we would have had a long, bloody civil war," a voice from the far back declared as Drew Weinstein got up to leave. "The Canadian government did the responsible thing—playing midwife to a split that had been inevitable from our founding." Weinstein paused in the corridor to hear the retort.

"That's a complete misreading of what happened," Brooks said. "Without outside meddling, the situation would have been resolved politically—"

"Like the Civil War?" A voice from the back said sarcastically, drawing hoots of approval from others.

"You might all want to think about the issues and dynamics of what's going on," Weinstein told the group from the doorway. "We can discuss it further before we leave on the trip... If that's good news, I'm about to hear."

The girl at the door prodded, "They are expecting you."

The waiting area in the Regional Agent for Travel's office consisted of two couches facing each other across a coffee table with a neat array of newspapers and magazines. A young man working at a desk outside the closed double doors to the inner office nodded to acknowledge Weinstein's arrival. "He's just finishing a call," he said. Moments later, both doors swung open, and the man motioned Weinstein inside. He was a short man, barely five feet tall, with dark hair and a deep-set, wrinkled face. He guided Weinstein toward a sitting area in front of floor-to-ceiling windows with a view of the city's main square below, where an early snow had left patches of white on the sidewalks.

"This must be a crazy time for you," Weinstein said to break the ice.

The Regional Agent, known among his colleagues for his humorless demeanor, shrugged. "We've all got things to deal with." He looked out the window and noted a few clouds in the sky. "I've been reading about how people dealt with the Great Depression," he continued. "They survived on pluck. People paid each other with IOUs. A lot took on boarders. They adapted to difficult times and were unbowed. People just did what they had to do to make things work." Weinstein looked past him to the books on the shelves running along one office wall. The man was a fellow historian, a scholar of Latin American history, focusing on Cuba. He followed Weinstein's gaze to the bookshelves. "Disruption is the norm, you know," he said, in all societies."

"I suppose that's right," Weinstein answered.

"Of course, it is," the Regional Agent said. "The elites in Cuba didn't see it coming. Russia, Afghanistan, Iran, the Soviet Union, Syria

—how many times have we seen seemingly stable societies completely upended?" Weinstein knew better than to interrupt him. "Venezuela," he added. "The gem of South America."

"The Separation caught the politicians and other leaders in our country by surprise," Weinstein said.

The Regional Agent gave a gruff laugh. "That's no shock," he said. "If you study ingrown toenails long enough, you forget they're part of the foot. Our leaders were too interested in things that weren't important in the long run, such as gender labels. We missed the rise of China, the collapse of the Soviet Union, the election of Trump."

"I'm hoping to give my group a broader view of the world," Weinstein said, steering the conversation to the proposed trip.

"You want to take them to Florida," the man said.

"A close friend of mine lives and works in the Panhandle. She's invited us."

"And you can get the paperwork?"

"There are a lot of catch-22s," Weinstein explained. "We can get the travel passes if we have an official invitation. But they'll only issue the invitation if we have approval from our State Department—that kind of thing."

"It would be a unique experience for your travelers," the Regional Agent said. "Frankly, it makes everyone look good—like we're more innovative than we really are." Weinstein felt a small burst of euphoria as he realized the trip would be approved. "I have one request," he continued. Weinstein waited for the man to lay out his terms, recognizing that request and demand were synonymous in the moment. "I'd like to send someone from the communications office to document your experience," the man said. "The PR people will love it."

The flight from Mexico City to Tallahassee took longer than expected due to disruptions in the air traffic control network. "We had to fly two sides of a triangle today, folks," the pilot explained after they landed. As the plane taxied to the international arrivals area, the travelers peered eagerly out the windows, knowing that nothing would look obviously different but still disappointed when that proved to be the case. The passengers deplaned and followed signs down a long corridor with tall windows looking out on the tarmac. At the bottom of an escalator, more signs pointed to different lines. The travelers veered right (PASSPORT HOLDERS OF THE FORMER UNITED STATES), after which laminated signs resting against orange construction cones indicated additional forks: TEXAS; CALIFORNIA AND THE PACIFIC STATES; INDIAN NATIONS; NEW ENGLAND; NATION OF THE ROCKIES; PLAINS-LAND. Weinstein ushered the group into the New England line behind two men in suits who were speaking to each other in hushed tones. Weinstein could see that they were carrying the forest-green provisional diplomat passports that had been issued to the representatives of the various regions in the immediate aftermath of the Separation.

At the front of the New England line, a large man in a bulging white shirt with a short red tie was sitting on a stool in front of a wooden podium with an open laptop. He waved the two diplomats through and then began typing slowly on his computer as if he had not seen the group of travelers lined up behind them. Eventually, he looked up. "Are you all together?"

"Yes," Weinstein answered. He stepped forward and handed the man a stack of light-blue travel certificates. The official flipped through them slowly. "Tourists," he said flatly.

"It's a group trip of informed travelers," Weinstein replied.

"From where?" the passport official asked. Weinstein named the city and described the purpose of the visit. The group members crowded anxiously behind him.

The official looked up at the group members. "You're here to tell us how to run our country," he said.

"We're here to learn about your new country," Weinstein said.

"Because those days of other people telling us how to run our country are over," the passport official continued.

"We're here to get a better grasp of what the future holds," Weinstein said.

"Wall Street and Washington won't be picking our pockets anymore," the official said. Weinstein recognized the talking point and nodded noncommittally. Some of the group members exchanged sly looks, acknowledging that the debt and entitlement negotiations underway in Denver would likely saddle this man's new country with decades of decisions that had been made in Washington and New York.

"Okay, go ahead," the official said. He waved the group through with the stack of travel certificates and then handed them back to Weinstein.

While the group members were waiting for their baggage to appear, Jonathan Brooks spotted a sign across the large arrivals hall. "Sick," he said loudly enough for the others to hear. Brooks hustled toward the sign, with several others following closely behind. Weinstein and the communications person, an officious former journalist in her early thirties, rushed to catch up. Brooks and the others following him reached the other side of the arrivals hall and immediately began taking photos with their phones. "I'm not sure we're supposed to be taking pictures here," Weinstein warned.

"Maybe just one with the whole group," the communications staffer suggested. "Let's get half the group on one side of the sign and half on the other side."

As the group arranged themselves clumsily for the photo, a female customs official in a blue polyester uniform walked briskly toward them. "Hold on," she said. "Hold on. There are no phones or cameras allowed until you are on the other side of customs." She was an older African American woman who seemed more bored by the group's transgression than angry.

"Sorry about that," Weinstein said.

"Where are you all from?" the customs official asked.

"New England," Weinstein answered.

"And you chose to come here?" she asked in a tone that invited laughter from the group. "Let me see your papers." Weinstein handed her the stack of light-blue documents. The woman whistled. "This is an educational tour?" she declared. "Are you going to fix this mess?"

"That's a tall order," Weinstein said.

"Maybe you can take me home with you," she said. The group members laughed. "I wanted to go north when all this went down, but I couldn't sell my house, and I didn't have enough assets to get a relocation permit." The group looked at each other uncomfortably.

"Our city lost many residents," Weinstein said.

"A whole lot of nonsense, that's what this is," the woman said. "You'd think we'd learned our lesson. You're gonna fix it, right?"

"We'll do what we can," Weinstein assured her.

The communications staffer asked, "Would you mind if we took just one picture in front of the sign?"

The customs official looked around the hall. "Make it quick," she said.

The students resumed their pose. "Drew Weinstein, can you get in the photo," the communications staffer instructed. "Tighter, everyone."

"Smiles or no smiles?" one of the group asked.

"Let's make this one serious," the communications staffer said. She snapped the photo with a large Nikon and immediately studied the image on the back of the camera. "That's perfect," she pronounced.

The group gathered their luggage and took it to where the group would board the bus to get to the city center. As the group was boarding the bus, the communications staffer added a short post to the travel blog the agency had created to promote the trip: "First Tourists Arrive for Historic Visit."

She quickly typed two sentences describing the day's travel and then uploaded the photo of Drew Weinstein posed with the group around the sign in the arrivals hall: WELCOME TO THE NEW CONFEDERATE STATES OF AMERICA.

A CASUALTY OF
THE DRUG WARS

After her sister, Nilda, died, Sofia began sleeping at the hospital. She returned home just once a week to wash her clothes, check the mail, and do little else. There was no reason to return to her apartment since she had no relatives after Nilda passed on. And there was no need to wash many clothes since she mostly wore hospital scrubs anyway, and the hospital provided those. She was a second-year resident at Los Angeles County-USC Medical Center. She worked eighty-plus hours a week and spent most of her time reading science fiction novels or watching Spanish language T.V. shows, soap operas, or other escapist entertainment.

Sofia came to America on a scholarship from the state of Durango in Mexico and completed pre-med studies and four years of medical school at USC. As a freshly minted M.D., she was in her second year of a four-year residency program in orthopedic medicine. Afterward, she will return to Mexico to practice medicine, her obligation under the scholarship grant.

She sleeps on a cot in a small room next to the trauma unit or at least tries to, since her sleep is usually interrupted after two or three hours, either by someone waking her to see the next critical patient received or by her own fitful dreams.

Some days she goes without sleep, kept awake by the near-constant activity of the trauma unit or the cries of family members of patients. The line between what she dreams and what she experiences daily tends to blur sometimes. And her mind and body are in a constant state of fatigue, whether on her cot attempting to rest or on duty standing over another victim of a gunshot wound or a body mangled in a car crash, knowing she is awake because she could dream nothing like this.

"A man is waiting there to see you," a nurse says. Sofia, who just laid down on the cot for only minutes, hoping to catch at least a few hours of sleep, rubs the weariness from her eyes.

"About what?"

The nurse hesitates. "He's right outside, and he didn't say what it was about. Only that it was a personal matter."

A minute later, in the hallway, the man introduces himself. "My name is Armando." He speaks English but with a heavy Spanish accent. She considers speaking to him in Spanish, but Sofia feels more comfortable conversing in English now.

A short beard descends from Armando's face. For a moment, she thinks he's a gay man, as that is a signature feature on those she works with that are gay. Then she notices by his scent that he hasn't bathed in quite a while or shaved, which is why his beard has grown out that way.

"I have something to tell you about your sister," he says. "Something terrible... something I did to her... something I am very sorry for."

"What is it?" Replies Sofia.

"Here? You want me to tell it here?"

"Yes." Then, given the anguish on his face, she says, "Or maybe we can go to the cafeteria, in the basement. There shouldn't be many people there at this hour."

The man nods, and Sofia says, "This way," pointing down a corridor where they go silently down to the elevators, passing newly injured arrivals, too many to care for by those still on duty. Sofia shakes her head. Maybe she should have asked him to tell her what he wanted outside the trauma unit.

"Do you want something?" She asks when they reach the cafeteria. Then she thinks she shouldn't have asked him because it would take too long and prolong his visit.

"Coffee and maybe a sandwich, please," he says. "If you have something," he adds with a smile.

"I can't because I need to get back, but I'll get you whatever you want." As she says that, his mood darkens, and her voice falters, her justification failing.

They go through the cafeteria line, and she gets tea and a scone, and he orders the daily special, meatloaf and potatoes, plus coffee. They go to a far corner a distance away from the only two other patrons near the entrance.

"I wanted to go into medicine as a paramedic or nurse," Armando says, switching to Spanish. "In my final year of high school, I applied but couldn't find a way to pay for it. I still hope to do that someday." He talked as he ate and finished his meal in under a minute.

"Of course, I tried to come here on a scholarship as you had but wasn't able to," he said. "Only a few can do that, the ones with brains or those with money, and I didn't have either."

Sofia looked at the wall clock. "I can't spend too much time with you. Tell me what you came here to say to me."

Armando looks down and, with his hand holding tightly to the table, says, "I... I killed your sister."

"What?" Sofia says, "But I was with her when she died... here, in the hospital, six weeks ago."

"But I did it. I was responsible for…." His voice trailed off, and he started weeping uncontrollably.

Sofia put her hand on his arm. She could feel the emotions running through his body. She would let him finish crying before she asked him anything else.

Six months earlier, Sofia received a call from someone at ICE, Immigration and Customs Enforcement, that her sister, Nilda, was at a holding facility after being apprehended by authorities. She was ill and needed medical care before being released to a family member.

Weeks later, when Sofia went to pick up Nilda, she couldn't believe how healthy her sister looked. She hugged her sister and joked about the padding on her hips. Whatever horrors Nilda had experienced in crossing the border, she'd put fat around her waist. "I am safe now," Nilda said, "Finally! And back with you," holding the hug longer than Sofia thought necessary.

They ate dinner that night, tamales, Nilda's favorite food, drank Mexican beer, and talked for hours about their times growing up in their hometown of Presidios before they finally went to bed. Sofia showed her sister to the spare room, gestured to the bed. "This is the place where you can sleep, Nilda."

They spent the next week in a state of heightened civility. No prying questions. All talk was small talk. What Sofia noticed, she did not comment on: a bottle of Ribavirin antiviral pills on the bathroom sink, cigarette burns on Nilda's shoulders, and several small scars on her face and hands. Sofia worked at the hospital, and Nilda worked on sleeping. Sofia brought food home each night from a Mexican restaurant specializing in regional dishes from their home state of Durango, and Nilda ate it. Sofia was up early each day to do the housekeeping before leaving for the hospital. She loved looking into the room where Nilda slept. This is wonderful, Sofia thought, to be with my sister again.

Ten years earlier, on the morning of September 19, 1994, the day the drug wars reached her hometown, Sofia woke in the Pardee Tower residence hall at the University of Southern California. She ate a quick breakfast of instant coffee and a day-old bran muffin, the latter by now her favorite American food. A few puffy clouds lined the horizon, but it was otherwise bright blue skies as she went down the stairs from her shared room and walked across the campus to the Stauffer Science Lecture Hall.

She attended a nationally renowned neurosurgeon lecture and took pride in her ability to follow the snaking sentences of foreign academia. Adjacent to the campus was the Natural History Museum of Los Angeles, with a section dedicated to the history of anatomy and pathology.

After thanking the lecturer and pausing in the atrium for a cigarette, she walked through the museum's curious exhibitions. A display was detailing the history of non-Egyptian mummification- an alcove dedicated entirely to the tibia. One room remained stuck in her memory, or her memory in it.

The room exhibited a collection of the 1,474 skulls collected by nineteenth-century physician Joseph Barnard Davis. A fractured skull of a Roman woman was found in the ruins of Pompeii. The skulls of five stillborns, each collapsed just above the temple. The skulls of nine Chinese pirates hanged in Ningpo. Aborigines from Tasmania. Congolese from Leopold's rubber mines.

But the skull that Sofia remembered was that of a Bengali cannibal. Fully intact, the mandible still locked against the temporal, the twenty-two bones that constitute the human skull all accounted for. The eight bones forming the neurocranial braincase bathed in halogenated light. From the size of the plates, the prominence of certain supra-orbital ridges and temporal lines, and the overall size and solidity of the skull, Sofia could tell it belonged to a man. The skull looked no different from those of the Chinese pirates, the Tasmanian Aborigines. The nose and eyes, which once gave the man physical distinction, were dark cavities. She read the placard, written by a Victorian phrenologist. There are no characteristics to distinguish the cranium of a cannibal from that of an ordinary man.

Sofia had felt at home there among the artifacts for the first time in her life.

Nilda slept for sixteen hours a day after arriving from Mexico. Sofia worried about her and didn't need a medical degree to know something was wrong. Nilda had been with her for fourteen days and had spent ten of those asleep.

"You must do something, go somewhere," Sofia said at breakfast. They never discussed Nilda's time spent coming north.

"There is nothing to do, nowhere to go."

"Go for a walk, then."

"I may get lost."

"Just don't go too far. Go in circles if you must. But you should get your daily exercise."

Sofia spent most of that day in surgery. Two children came in after being involved in a traffic collision. They were thrown from the car because they didn't have seat belts on. They didn't survive the surgery.

Nilda's eyes were red when Sofia arrived home.

"Why are you crying?" she asked.

"I went for a walk and thought I saw Jaime in the street. Remember him? How we could talk and laugh together. Then she burst out laughing."

Sofia slapped her sister across the face. How could she laugh once again like that? Nilda stopped crying and didn't seem surprised. As they ate in silence, the bruise on her cheek grew to a crimson swell.

A constellation of vital phenomena, Sofia thought. Tomorrow it would look worse, but Nilda would live. Sofia couldn't pity her, not after what memories she had aroused. Before she went to bed, Sofia put some crushed ice in a plastic bag and placed it outside her sister's door. Sofia knocked and, before the door opened, went back to her room.

Nilda never forgot the admiration with which her sister had spoken of going to school in the United States. Nilda applied to the same universities as Sofia, and the same scholarships, but without Sofia's superior test scores. After completing high school, Nilda had a job as a clerk in a department store, a steady boyfriend, Friday nights at the movies or the dance club, and a radio that played the latest hip-hop tunes. Life was okay, and she looked forward to getting married and having children. Then came the drug wars, and everything changed. There were killings on the streets, people disappearing, shootings almost daily in the malls, restaurants, and theaters.

An aunt raised Sofia and Nilda after their parents died of food poisoning while attending a wedding when they were pre-teens. When the aunt died a year after Sofia left, Nilda remained. She went to live with a girlfriend, but she married soon after. Living alone for Nilda was not bad, but she was lonely on occasion. And there were always men to take her out. While she wasn't as bright as her sister, she was beautiful. Sofia may have once been the most promising medical student in all of her home state of Durango, but no one had ever turned to watch her as she walked down the street. Nilda reminded herself of this and used it to countervail her envy. Sofia was in America, and Nilda thought she wouldn't return. They hadn't spoken in years, not since the day in September 2001 when Sofia called her after the 9/11 terrorist attack on the Twin Towers in New York took the lives of almost 3000 people.

On 9/11, communication tie-ups made it almost impossible to make any calls between the two countries. Nilda thought she might call and check on how her sister was doing but decided not to. She was safe; her ugly sister with a big brain was a long distance from New York. Nilda thought she was at greater risk, and Sofia should be calling her often to check on how she was doing. That's what Nilda told her when she called.

"Yes, I am surviving here, and that's no thanks to you," Nilda told her. "It's a lot worse than twenty 9/11's put together. We passed the 100,000 mark for deaths and missing long ago. Here in Durango alone, the toll is over 10,000. And I survived it fine. I can do that because I am beautiful. At times like this, that's better than brains."

And that was true. The drug wars made everything physical: survival, retaliation, even comfort. Avenues existed for women who could make themselves attractive, but which brought its own negative consequences.

Armando Vargas was two years ahead of Nilda at school and not someone she was interested in. He had compressed features as if, as a child, he'd been hit in the face with a frying pan. Even so, he had loved Nilda almost from the moment he first saw her in school. She never dated him, but she had dated several of his friends and came to be someone she liked as a friend, just not as a boyfriend.

She sat with him in a bar one day, waiting to join several others. The subject of her sister came up. "You want to get out like her? Who doesn't?" he said.

"I do. I know I can be successful there. Just look at me. I could be a movie star."

Armando pursed his lips. "Anyone can be successful when they are not dodging bullets." He pulled a plastic water bottle from his jacket pocket and scanned the room before taking a quick sip. "Real good tequila from my uncle Esteban's cabinet," he said. "Want to try some?"

"He's the trafficker, isn't he?"

Armando was taken aback by the remark. "Yes, he does that sometimes."

"How much? What does it cost now to be taken across?"

Was she seriously thinking of that? Maybe she was just curious. "Why do you ask? It used to be one hundred thousand pesos, maybe more now. But you haven't any money."

"I have a little, and once I'm there, I will work off the debt."

"Will you?"

"Of course. I'm hard working... and can be trusted. And if your uncle won't do it for me, I know there are trafficking routes and traffickers along the way. Just look at me. Don't you think I can persuade someone to help me get across?"

Armando shook his head. "You are a beautiful girl, Nilda, but you are a poor girl in a poor country that is having problems right now. Once you get to America, it might go okay for you. But getting there safely is the problem. It used to be that a girl who disappeared needed to reappear on the other side of the border to make money. Now, they just disappear. Reappearance has too high an overhead. Kidnappings, abductions, these are national industries now."

Nilda stood to leave. Money paled against the desire to simply leave this country. She didn't care if a pot of gold sat on the other side. She just wanted to get over the rainbow. "Wait," Armando said. He paused to consider what to say next to her. He cared for her and wanted to make sure no harm came to her. Yet, she seemed determined to go. "You are a friend. We went to school together, no? And stayed friends ever since. When do you want to go?"

"Right now," Nilda responded. "I would leave with the clothes I'm wearing and not look back."

"Then I will help you. I have some money and will give it to my uncle to take you to the border, where he will turn you over to a coyote specializing in family crossings. Do you know what those are?"

Nilda shook her head.

"It's a way the coyotes get around problems. The coyotes give you $1,000 to cross the Rio Grande and seek asylum — but only if you take a child with you and you surrender to the U.S. Border Patrol on the other side. Otherwise, it would cost $5,000 to have them lead you across the last five miles or so and then evade the migras at the border and the interior checkpoints beyond.

"So I am to play the part of a mother. Do I look like a mother to you?"

Armando smiled. He would love to have her be the mother of his children. "Yes, something like a mother… a very pretty one, of course."

"And the other way, without taking a child across, would a coyote trust me to pay later?"

"Yes, I think so, of course."

It was Armando's smile, more than his words, that Nilda mistrusted. Did he really know that was true, or was he just telling her what she wanted to hear? "I'm not my sister, but I'm not a fool."

"There may be other things you can do to pay off the debt. Dancing. Entertaining. And also being… what's the word, enticing."

Nilda knew it meant prostitution. Even if she had to do that for a while, Nilda thought, so what? Does he think I am afraid of it? I've been with many men; what's a few more if it means I get to America?

"Okay," she said. "Help me get across. Have me disappear here and make me reappear there."

Another man, not Armando's uncle, transported Nilda with six other women in a truck to the small fishing village of Los Mochis. From there, they took a local fishing trawler, arriving at a pier sixty kilometers south of Mexicali. Two of the women stayed with the trawler, which would go on to Ensenada. Nilda and the three others went with two men in a transport truck. The back door slammed shut. When it opened again, they were in Mexicali. She spent the first night in a stone cellar with ten other women, half still girls, the youngest no older than twelve. "Where am I?" she asked the closest one in Spanish. The woman responded in Bulgarian. Nilda asked again in English. "The breaking grounds," the woman said. Nilda didn't understand. What ground was to be broken? They were in a cellar, already underground. She looked at her dirty clothes, the soil rubbed against her palms, and understood. She was the ground, and she was to be broken.

Sofia tried to spend as much time as she could at her place now that Nilda was with her. She would rush back from the hospital in hopes that she would be awake. But most times, she wasn't. She tried to sleep as well, but there was always something to do when she got home. And at the hospital, the work was almost non-stop. Sofia takes amphetamines to stave off sleep.

A man is carried in, a gunshot wound with the bullet still lodged in his chest. He's dead before reaching the surgery table, but Sofia still treats the wound. She undresses him, pulls the lethal projectile from between his ribs, then cleans and bandages the gash. Four stitches to close the wound. At least he'll be presentable when his next of kin have to identify him.

Another gunshot wound victim, someone she's attended to before. How many times? More than twice. The streets of Los Angeles rival those of her hometown sometimes. "You must return in ten days so I can remove the stitches," Sofia says aloud. "If you see any pus, any sign of infection, you must return at once." If he doesn't return, then he surely will when he's shot again.

She examines the rest of his body. Why do they all have poor personal hygiene? "You must bathe more often," she tells him, "and shake powder on the toes to alleviate your athlete's foot. If you don't, you risk becoming the victim of foot fungus."

She works her way back up the body, pausing at the torso to ask the man's weight, quizzing him on his diet. "You must eat more fruits and vegetables, not just beans and tortillas," she says.

She looks at his face, cradles the man's cheeks between her palms, and speaks to his deadened eyes. "I will give you a prescription for that skin infection. Two applications should clear it up." Was he even listening? She thinks back to something she read: There are no characteristics to distinguish the cranium of a cannibal from that of an ordinary man. Then she adds: But from observing the length of your supraorbital ridge, I can ascertain that you are most certainly an asshole.

Two hands on her shoulders gently nudge her awake. It's Nilda, and she is smiling. "You must have been dreaming," she says. "About what? You were mumbling something."

"That's not important," Sofia says. Nilda's breath is warm against her neck. "What's important is that you're looking better."

Sofia tries to get up, but Nilda pushes her back into her bed. "You must rest," she commands.

"Don't tell me what to do. I'm the doctor here, not you. And I'm not tired."

"You've been working for almost three days straight. Who do you think you are, Superwoman?"

"I think I am someone who slept last night, for a few hours at least, at the hospital. Here, I have trouble falling asleep."

Nilda goes to the book closet, scans the disordered stack, and picks a thick volume. "Read this if you need help falling asleep," she says, handing her a medical dictionary.

Sofia lifts the dictionary. The binding creaks like rusty hinges as she opens the cover. The book closet is rarely opened, and she's surprised Nilda even knows of its existence. Surgeons don't consult the medical textbooks. They learn their craft as a glasscutter learns his. Most lessons from medical school have proven irrelevant. Lectures didn't cover multiple gunshot wounds.

"I'll fix breakfast later today. You lie back and try to get some sleep," Nilda says.

Sofia dozes off with the dictionary open on her lap. The sleep isn't real, isn't slumber, only a fitfulness exacerbated by the comedown from amphetamines. Dehydration, exhaustion, poor nutrition, depletion of serotonin. She knows the symptoms but can't explain them in her dreams.

Sofia wakes up to an amphetamine hangover: headache, dry mouth, accelerated heart rate. She goes out for a smoke, pulling a white filtered Marlboro from the pack. She smokes two or three cigarettes a week. She received a carton as a gift months ago and just finished the first pack last week. A few deep inhalations, the carbon soaking into her capillaries. Cancer is not a concern, not with so few cigarettes. Nilda walks out a few minutes later, her hands wrapped around a cup of tea.

"I overheard you on the phone yesterday," he says. "You were speaking English without an accent. You are indeed an Americana now."

"A Scottish friend of mine. He said Durango was in the British news today." Sofia smiles. "Imagine that. Of course, it was about the cartels. What else?"

"How is it you know someone from Scotland?"

"He went to medical school at USC for three years and then transferred to London."

"He's in London now?" Nilda seemed impressed. "I've always wanted to visit there. It's… historical. The land of Robin Hood, the Knights of the Round Table, Camelot, and Shakespeare."

Sofia smiled. "I left my sister when she was only interested in boys and clothes, and now English history?"

"I'm now no longer sixteen, or haven't you noticed?"

"You've grown, in many ways." Sofie turned serious. "You know, I've tried to keep up with what you were doing, even when we weren't talking. I learned you headed north to cross the border, but I didn't hear from you after that, and I was worried. Every day I thought about you and even cried some times. You left home, and I didn't know if you were alive or dead. It was like you had been disappeared. But you hadn't. I was so relieved and happy when I got a call about you."

"I didn't know that."

"Family is a good thing, an important thing always. So is home. I think of home sometimes too… Presidios, and all of Durango. It's lovely in the Spring. Did you know Frida Kahlo and Leon Trotsky once traveled to Durango? He wrote about it."

"Who are they?"

"Nilda, you must read more about Mexico, if nothing else."

"I'm sorry if I am less than you in everything. I didn't come here to be reminded of that."

"I'm sorry… I didn't mean to upset you."

Nilda sighed. "No, I don't you do that on purpose. But you do it all the same. Back home and here."

"I'm sorry, I really am."

"Anyway, home is not the same." Nilda has a vision. She remembers the street just outside a cafe on the main square where she and her friends would go. A heavily armored pick-up truck filled in the back with cartel members armed with automatic weapons rumbles over the asphalt and stops near the cafe. As it does, it is fired upon by a group of similarly armed men as she and her friends scramble to get away and hide. Ten minutes later, the firefight is over, and none of the armed men are left standing. An older woman comes out of an alley pulling a cart, pausing every few feet to collect whatever she can to sell later. No, home is not the same.

"Do you remember Jovita?" Nilda says finally.

"Jovita Gomez? Yes, of course, she was in your class and a good friend of yours. It's tragic what happened to her."

Nilda nods.

"First Jovita, then her husband. And I'm told that even her sister Josie has disappeared."

"Yes, and many more in their families."

"By which cartel? Zetas or Sinaloa?" Sofia asks.

"Neither. They've been disappeared by another cartel entirely." Nilda studies Sofia. Does she appreciate what's happened since she left?

"Why Jovita? She's only a girl."

"Who knows." Nilda shrugs. "Perhaps she saw something, heard something, or they just think she did. It doesn't matter why."

"I heard you and she were no longer friends. That she hadn't talked to you in years."

"She matters, and all her family matters because home matters."

"I didn't mean anything by that," Sofia says, but Nilda is already walking away.

The morning after Sofia hit her sister, she made excessive noise while brewing coffee. She banged pots into each other, dropped one pan then another. She wanted to make sure Nilda was awake before she knocked.

"Nilda," Sofia called quietly through the cracked door. "You must wake up."

Nilda's face had swollen overnight, a patch of deep purple stitched to her cheekbone. She didn't meet Sofia's eyes.

"You must come to the hospital," Sofia said. "There is a little open wound by your eye, and you don't want it to become infected."

"I am not afraid of that."

"You should be. You have a beautiful face and don't want it to be spoiled in any way."

Nilda glared. For a moment, Sofia worried Nilda would invoke the past. The brothels, the pimps, the beatings. And to be struck by her own sister. Was Sofia no better? She dismissed the question as soon as she asked it. And why? Because blood is thicker than water, and guilt is thickest of all.

"Fine," Nilda said. "Let's go."

At the hospital, Sofia dressed the wound with antiseptic ointment. She softly rubbed the cream across the flesh, blowing it dry. That was her apology. A few patients waited for treatment, but nothing urgent. A case of the flu. A sprained ankle. Sofia saw no gunshot wounds all morning. It was a good day.

She decided to take Nilda on a brief tour of the hospital. They walked through the various wards and laboratories, and she pointed out the purposes of each. "This is one of the foremost oncology departments in the entire U.S.," Sofia said as they passed through a wing filled with people, purpose, and function. "Famous people from all the world come for treatment." They paused at a hulking MRI machine. "It is the latest in technology, and the cost was astronomical, but it is worth it. It can detect cancer better than anything else."

The tour ended at the maternity ward. A woman had given birth the previous night. Her child was born with a collapsed lung, but the doctor on call acted quickly, and the child lived. The mother held the infant to her breast. She beamed as Nilda and Sofia approached.

"She will live," the mother said, shaking her head with disbelief. She looked at Nilda, taking her for a nurse. "I'm so glad you are here."

Nilda glanced at Sofia. "I am just walking through."

"Nonsense," the mother said. "You save lives."

Nilda smiled. The baby finished suckling and looked upward.

"Do you want to hold her?" the mother asked.

"No."

"Nonsense," the mother said. "Of course, you want to hold her."

"I must go, but you stay here," Sofia whispered as Nilda took the infant in her arms. "There is always someone in need of my urgent attention."

After she was broken, the handlers sold Nilda to a brothel just outside Tijuana, which catered to the tourists coming over from San Diego nearby. Breaking—the hypodermic of heroin, the gang rape, the auction block.

A month passed, and someone else purchased her with three others and took them south to Ensenada. There they were offered to tourists coming off cruise ships. Nilda was sold three more times, but certain things remained constant. Each morning she was injected with heroin. By afternoon she was itching. By evening she was willing to perform as required to ensure a shot later that night.

She knew: she would be killed if she fled, she would be arrested if she went to the police, she would be found if she went home. She did not know where she was, what language was spoken to her, where to get money, or how to get home.

It felt like autumn, but maybe it was Spring. She once saw ancient Maya ruins, great stone pillars, walls without roofs. Or did she imagine that? Days passed without distinction. Time was marked not by minutes but by men. Eight one night, eleven the next. Each felt like a porcupine between her legs. Men from the factories, the ranches, the shops, and tourists. College boys, older men, even young boys. Men from the U.S., Mexico, Italy, and Germany. Fat men, skinny men, balding, graying, and wheezing men. They called her Maria, and she didn't understand why. Then another woman told her: That's what any girl is called. We're all Marias.

An average day consisted of ten men, three cheeseburgers, four glasses of tap water, and two shots. A toothbrush, no toothpaste. Weeks without tasting fresh air. The first woman had been right. Modern-day slavery, but there was nothing modern about it.

The days passed, but they were all nights. On the fifteenth floor of an apartment high-rise, locked doors, and windows. Eight Marias in total. Four bunk beds crammed into the bedroom. Fucked on a king-sized bed, falling asleep on a lower bunk. One Maria died. Seven Marias left. A new Maria arrived to fill in the eighth bunk. They were all interchangeable. All replaceable and all disposable.

The pimp was from her home state of Durango, said his mother had lost the use of her legs in the first firefight in Presidios and that he needed to make money to keep her safe and comfortable. Was that reason enough to make Nilda's life a living hell?

The belt around the bicep, the two taps on the syringe, the blood pulled into the barrel, the push of the plunger, the moment of peace. The threat of being beaten with electrical wires. The meals from Burger King and KFC, the slices of pizza. The junkie dreams crowd into daylight.

Nilda went with Sofia to the hospital each morning. She said she wanted to be helpful, work as a volunteer, a greeter, or anything else that was available. Word got around, and she found a paid position in the maternity ward. The head of pediatrics gladly put her to work to help the nurse's helpers. She fed newborns and disinfected instruments. She scrubbed bedpans, washed sheets. She slept less and began keeping the same schedule as Sofia.

Sofia dropped by the maternity ward during downtime and always found Nilda busy. She could not sit still, could not not be working. When she completed everything asked of her, she asked to do more. Sofia didn't know if Nilda could bear children, if she could ever again let a man touch her. But she could do this, Sofia thought, peeking through the door as Nilda hushed a newborn to sleep. The infant in her arms would learn to live in this world, and so too would Nilda. Sofia believed this, and she shut the door and returned to the trauma ward.

The Acapulco vice police shut down the brothel, arresting everyone there after a sensational article in an American newspaper told of prostitution at that location. Modern Day Slavery in Mexico it was titled and said, "Nearly 20,000 Mexican women are trafficked and forced into sex work in tourist centers like Acapulco and Cancun, and border cities like Tijuana and Mexicali.

We visited one such location that catered to tourists off cruise ships….” Nilda spent a week in jail on prostitution and indecency charges before being transferred to a clinic specializing in victims of human trafficking.

The woman psychiatrist sat behind a desk and spoke Spanish in a lisping Castilian accent. Her syllables seemed in danger of fluttering away. The questions she asked sounded simple but could not be answered.

“What happened?”

“How did you get here?”

“Are you okay?”

Nilda tried to respond but kept stumbling over her words.

“It’s fine. Everything is fine,” the woman said. “Just start at the beginning.”

“The beginning?” Nilda laughed. There was no beginning. “My sister won a scholarship to study in America, and everyone was so fucking proud of her.”

Within two months, Nilda had finished her program of methadone maintenance treatment. She still took Ribavirin antiviral, still needed it for another thirty-six weeks to wipe out the hepatitis C. She never opened the envelope containing the results of the HIV test. Her request for immediate entry into the U.S. for a reunion with her sister was denied. The psychiatrist said she would speak with the immigration officials and would give a strong recommendation for reunification. Still, in the end, all she could secure for Nilda was a six-month supply of Ribavirin. She would have to return to Presidios.

On the way to the airport, something unusual happened. She didn’t understand what or why, but when asked by the customs official what city her sister lived in so that she would get on the right plane, she answered Los Angeles. Then she was given a ticket to that destination and documents as a war refugee. Was this a mistake? Her hands were clammy as her fingers pinched the corner of the travel pass as the official stamped and scanned the document. She had no luggage. The planes looked like big metal birds. Graceful creatures incapable of harm. She had never been on a plane; now, one would take her to her sister in Los Angeles.

A voice came over the intercom in a language she didn't understand. The cabin doors shut, and the plane taxied to the runway, the hum of the turbines going to a growl. The landscape smeared across the window, then liftoff. She watched the ground. The plane gained altitude, and the men below shrank to pinpricks, then they were gone altogether. She exhaled. The earth fell away. She was free of the drug wars and all that came with them.

MY DOG SKIPPY

The first dog I ever had was named Skippy. That was also the name of the last dog I ever had, or will ever have. To lose both was heartbreaking, and I never want to go through that again.

My first Skippy came to me when I was eight, and I lost him six months later. Or, I should say, he was taken away from me by my father because he would stop yelping while my father tried to sleep. "Out in the shed," he said, "and he'll stay there until he doesn't make a sound." That night we had the first winter storm of the season, and it was near freezing when my older brother went out to check on Skippy the following day.

"He's gone," Steve said when I asked about Skippy.

"Where'd he go," I said. "Aren't we going out to find him?"

"He's gone and never coming back... He's dead, froze to death, or knocked himself out trying to get out. I can't tell which."

"Maybe we can take him to the vet, to get him well again, don't you think?"

"Sure, I'll tell Dad that when he comes home tonight," Steve said and walked away. I later learned my father took Skippy, but not to the vet, and we never talked about Skippy again.

◆ ◆ ◆

It was about twenty years later when I found a dog, and I named him Skippy. Or Skippy found me, I should say. It was when I was driving downtown in my VW bus, it was rush hour, and the traffic stalled behind a long red light by an overpass.

Suddenly I look up at some kids who appear to be playing on top of the overpass, five or six boys, eleven or twelve years old. They're throwing stones at random cars, but then I see they are pushing this helpless dog over the guardrail. It all happens so fast—the dog falls onto the hood of the car in front of me and rolls into the street, screeching and crying out in pain. I jump out in the middle of traffic and yell at the boys: "What are you doing! Are you out of your minds?"

I run to the dog's side, pull him out of the traffic, and I take him back to my mini-bus and take him to the vet. His right front foot is broken in several places and has to be wrapped in a cast, but other than that, he isn't seriously injured, which is surprising. He's a very good dog, a medium-size collie with orange and white fur and beautiful, soulful eyes. He's already housebroken, and he stays at home in my apartment all day long, guarding it until I get home from work—without causing any trouble or commotion—then he limps out happily to greet me. I had to call him Skippy, of course.

Skippy had a fetching way of coming up to me while I was lying on the couch, putting his nose up close to my face, and staring intensely into my eyes. Then he raises his injured right paw as if he wants to shake hands. Of course, this tactic almost always works.

I take his paw in my hand, then hug him, pet his doggy head, and tell him what a wonderful dog he is. I tell him his hunting abilities are unsurpassed; I highly value his watchdog capabilities, and, in addition to that, he has a beautiful coat, a great nose, and a terrific personality. His eyes go glassy with contentment.

Skippy lived with me for three years, knitting himself into the fabric of my life. He was a companion, my best friend, and my confessor. I could tell him anything, and he never judged me, criticized me, or left me.

Skippy had been acting poorly, and I had the vet examine him. He gives me the dire opinion that there is no help for it—whether from his fall from the overpass and internal injuries or merely from old age or maladies associated with mongrel life on the lam —Skippy is going to die within days.

The vet offered to put him to sleep, but I said no—I don't want that. I wasn't convinced that Skippy was that ill. But if he was that ill, I think it is more humane to let him die at home. That's what I would want if I were a dog. But I actually think I might be able to save him. I'll pet him more often, and I'll fix a special place for him on the deck with a more comfortable bed and a bowl of his favorite dog food next to his water dish. I keep a close eye on him.

But Skippy didn't last a week.

He wouldn't eat unless I fed him very slowly and carefully with a spoon. After a couple of days, he wouldn't eat or drink at all. He looked terribly thin, and his head was hanging down in misery. He seemed glued to his bed, but when I picked him up to encourage him to walk a bit, he whined as if in pain. I began to realize that maybe the vet was right after all.

Skippy does have one bad habit that I could never cure him of, developed no doubt during his mysterious former life before me: he hates and distrusts the mailman so intensely that he has been a threat to our mail delivery. Monday through Saturday, without fail, even in his weakened condition, he throws a snarling, barking fit as soon as the mailman appears. He is absolutely fanatical about this. He can spot a mail truck from a block away, and, as far as he is concerned, it is a vehicle driven by the devil himself. I don't know how he developed this unreasonable prejudice against mailmen and mail trucks, but I suppose some mailman had once squirted him with dog repellent or kicked him or otherwise abused him in a way he considers unforgivable.

Sometime in the middle of the afternoon, he gets up and staggers down the steps and across the yard, and I am hopeful for a moment. But then I think that he is just trying to run away—to go off somewhere and die like an old elephant—so I call him. "Here, Skip-Skip-Skippy. Here, boy." When he ignores my call—which he has never done before—I run after him. His running is shaky and lopsided. I catch up with him in the parking lot of an apartment building down the block. I grab him and lift him up into my arms to carry him home, but he starts barking and screeching in such a crazy, panicky way that someone in the apartment building actually calls the police to report a disgusting incident of dog kidnapping or animal abuse. I hold Skippy and wait for a while in the grass at the edge of the road until he calms down.

The police—who must not have much to do this time of year—catch up with us just as I am turning into our yard, hugging Skippy to my chest, and the officer gets out of his cruiser and approaches us with a big revolver on one hip and a big billy club on the other. Skippy chooses this moment to start up a new high-pitched snarling and yipping fit—with what energy he has left—because, I realize too late, he thinks the cop is the mailman. I have to explain to the skeptical officer exactly where I am going with this animal and exactly who I am, and exactly who the dog is and why he is crying and moaning so hysterically. The policeman listens and grills me and finally gets it straight, and then he says, in a matter-of-fact way, that if the dog dies, I should be sure to call the animal control office to see that the body is disposed of properly. Then he drives away.

I carry Skippy up the steps to his bed, staying with him for several more hours until he dies. I decide I will bury my dog in my own backyard, even if it is an apartment building because this is his home, probably the only good home he ever had, and because I want to be able to visit his grave. None of the neighbors think this is a good idea at all, but I am beyond reasoning. Watching him die and pressing his dying body against my chest has left me feeling raw and inconsolable.

After dinner, in the twilight, I trudge out to the far back part of the yard and dig the grave next to a blue spruce in a place that looks like a comfortable spot to spend eternity. I inhale the musky scent of the loam as I dig, and I brood about Skippy's unrealized life—unloved until I rescued him and terrorized by hideous mailmen. Then, on the deck, I carefully wrap his body in a black plastic garbage bag, and feeling otherworldly, I pick him up and solemnly carry him down the stairs and out to the backyard. Lights are coming on around the neighborhood, and I worry that someone will see me and report me to the police.

But I really don't care—I can't think about that. I'm already crying when I say, "Good-bye, Skippy, you were always a good dog, and I'll never forget you," and I place the unwieldy bag into the darkness of the hole I carved. But feeling his body against me again and then feeling it go down into the hole, something in me snaps, and I start sobbing so loudly that a neighbor comes down, seizes me by the shoulders, and pulls me up. "Shhhhhh," she says. "You're going to alert the whole neighborhood. Cover him up now, and let's go back." But I can't move; I can't stop bawling. I don't care who hears me or who comes to arrest me. My dog Skippy is dead.

THE RED LION
FISH PARADOX

"**M**argie, you have the unique ability to look, to the outside world, utterly serene and unruffled, while, on the inside, all must be chaos," my father once said to me. That was often true, and this was one of those times.

When you're a Ph.D. student, not much is expected of you until you graduate. You get used to telling people that you'll start living an everyday life once you complete your studies in a breathless, self-righteous sort of way. And even though I found it grating to continue to say that into my thirties, eventually, I grew jealous of those who had started living their "normal" life.

I told myself that those who hadn't continued in college to get the maximum education available were doomed to be making $15 an hour in some dead-end job, living in a trailer on the edge of town, having three children because they got the maximum in food stamps, whether or not your husband worked steadily or not.

Still, six months after I had graduated, finally and barely, I hadn't landed the job that would pay more than minimum wage to start. Someone with a Women's Studies Major and a Minor in Environmental Studies isn't much in demand; I found out. Then, finally, I'd seen a posting for environmental justice enthusiasts who liked to travel, and I ripped the flyer from the café bulletin board. I applied and got the job. What was it exactly? I was to go to where people fished and work on drumming up interest in a fish called the Red lion.

I threw my bags into the back of my Subaru, slammed the trunk shut, got on I-70 East, and headed toward Reedville, West Virginia. The whole state was mine to choose from, and I decided on Reedville based on luck: I brought a map up of the state and, closing my eyes, I stuck a finger out, and it landed there.

I left Columbus, Ohio, and drove east for nearly eight hours, the flat roads flanked by pine forests and gas stations and billboards for plastic surgery and tanning beds. The monotony kept me from thinking, lulled my brain into an exhausted fog. I stopped and got an enormous iced tea, the condensation dripping down my wrist and onto the seat of the car.

I'd been studying the invasive Red Lion fish for the past six weeks in preparation for this trip. I'd always thought it an extraordinary-looking fish, scarlet red in color with a permanent frown and several dazzling, venomous appendages. Native to Brazil, the fish started appearing near Florida in the '90s—and now was destroying entire reef ecosystems. With no natural predators, they proliferate from Florida to West Virginia, releasing something like two million eggs a year.

My job was to convince people to start eating them. My boss at Invasivores, a new conservation organization, had given me a script. When I spoke to people, I was supposed to say: "We're creating a new generation of invasivores—people who hunt and eat invasive species in order to save native species. You can help save the planet by incorporating Red Lion into your diet!" When I spoke to "ordinary folks"—that's how they said it to me, as if that's a box you could check on a census—I was supposed to say, "Red Lions are plentiful, free, and they taste great—soft white flesh, like a hogfish. They're poisonous to the touch but great to eat."

I got closer to Bretz, the town just outside Reedville. Men sat motionless in the sun in front of pickup trucks parked on the roadsides; signs advertising sweet potatoes, collards, and live bait seemed ubiquitous. I felt uncomfortable with that new-kid feeling like I was starting at a school where I knew I wouldn't fit in.

A few minutes later, I pulled into a long, sandy driveway off a road called Old Lake House Road. I found a two-story blue duplex on stilts, perceptibly listing to one side. I knew without entering that it was going to smell like an ancient underwater cave, like mildew. Houses like these take on so much weather, like getting slapped in the face repeatedly by hurricane winds and high tides.

"Hey there, sailor," a tall, skinny man said. He came out from the utility closet underneath the house in denim cut-offs.

"Hey," I said, wondering if he had my name wrong or if "sailor" was a term of endearment. "I'm Margie, from Invasivores."

"I can tell," he said. "Let's get your stuff in the house before the weather breaks." He pointed at the charcoal-color cloud on the horizon.

A few other houses were on the road, but this wasn't a second-home hotspot like Arrowhead or Indian Springs. It felt authentic, and a little sad, like the remains that others had passed over.

"Ward Williams," he said, shaking my hand too hard. He scooped up a suitcase and two bags—he was wiry-looking but strong, maybe in his early fifties—and bounded up the wooden staircase to the first floor of the lake house.

Inside, the white paint was speckled with black mildew, and the drywall had some damp spots. He showed me to my room. "I'll let you get settled," he said, "and then we can meet up in the living room and talk logistics."

I smiled and closed the bedroom door, swallowing down the dread. I could just turn and leave, I thought to myself. Instead, I slung my bags into the corner of the room and arranged my toiletries on the rattan chest of drawers. Downstairs I could hear Ward bustling around in the living room and went to join him, afraid of being alone with my thoughts another minute.

"How'd you get into fish?" he asked, handing me a Coors Light.

Was I really even into fish? It was hard to say.

I cracked open the Coors and took a sip. "My dad kept two forty-gallon aquarium tanks in the waiting room of his dentist's office," I told him. "He used to pay me three dollars a week to clean them and arrange the faux coral in the bottom of the tank."

"Oh," Ward said, grinning. "You started off as one of the bad guys."

I laughed because he was right. It wasn't cool to talk about aquariums in conservation circles, not unless you were breeding natives or something earnest like that. In fact, it was thought that the Red Lion had first gotten into the waters around Miami after a hurricane wiped out an aquarium tank left unattended, sweeping the poisonous fish into the local waters.

Ward finished off his beer in a long gulp and opened another. "This was my mother's house," he said as if apologizing. "I never would have picked white carpet."

"I hear that," I said.

"Do you ever think, 'Man—how am I related to my parents?'" he said, shaking his head, taking another long sip of his beer.

"All the time," I said, thinking about the mother I never saw, who now sold cosmetics at a mall in Texas.

"But the thing is—the older you get, you just feel it in your bones," he said. "And in your words. Can you feel it?"

I must have cringed because he laughed. "But I've got a decade or two on you, sailor," he said. "You still have time to change so much that your ancestors can't catch up to you."

He stood up, walked to the fridge, and pulled out another beer.

"You may have assumed I have a drinking problem by now," he said. "And you'd be right. But I'm harmless. I sleep it off. Can I get you one before I turn in?"

I shook my head.

"See you in the morning, then."

I was left alone—me and a giant Catfish over the fireplace, an unlit cigarette cradled in its open mouth. I stared through the windows at the seemingly infinite darkness of the lake. Now that Ward was gone, I could hear the lapping of the water and the wind.

In the morning, I threw on a T-shirt and shorts, pulled my hair back, and set out to buy groceries. I found a local bait shop that offered pontoon boat tours, beer, and some dusty-looking packaged foods. I bought some soup, crackers, and Pop-Tarts, knowing I would eat all of the latter first before I touched anything else.

"Who are you out here visiting?" the clerk asked, eyeing me. She looked to be in her sixties, with leathery skin, a sweet smile, and blue eye shadow. A wall of cigarettes and lottery tickets was behind her head.

"I'm studying the Red Lion fish," I said. I liked how that sounded, even though it wasn't entirely true.

"Gross little devil fish!" she said, blinking her mascara-laden lashes. "What do you want to know about them?"

"Well," I said, taking a deep breath. "They're plentiful, free, and they taste great—soft white flesh, like a hogfish."

"They're poisonous," she said, giving me the eye. "Like being stung by a jellyfish, I've heard."

"True," I said. "But they're fine to eat."

"You can have them all for yourself, honey," she said, breaking into a smile. She put my groceries into a plastic bag.

"No bag for me," I said, beginning to empty the contents.

"You're one of those world-savers," she said, shaking her head. "Staying over at Ward's, I bet."

"Yes, ma'am," I said.

"We always know if a world-saver is in town, they've come to stay with Ward." She leaned down as if she was about to tell me a secret. "He's about half-cocked if you want to know the truth," she said. "His family's been big landowners around here for generations. But Ward's as crazy as the day is long, hell-bent on punishing himself for something he didn't do."

I nodded. I was curious but couldn't bring myself to ask for more details.

"You be safe," she said. The door chimed as I walked out with my armful of groceries.

It was already hot out, and the inside of my car felt oppressive. The air was thick. I drove back to Ward's with the windows down, passing a few roadside stands, people walking dogs. Folks out here looked tired, as if they were waiting for something better to happen but knew it wouldn't.

Congratulations, I thought, turning into Ward's driveway. You escaped the development boom, and now it's too late—everyone knows rising seas are going to wipe those lakefront places off the map. Here, in the interior, you will never have to deal with price-inflated condominiums, homeowner associations, and mini-golf. But I guess it's not much of a consolation to know that this is the best it's going to be. That better isn't coming.

I put the groceries on the shelves and in the mini-fridge in my room. I took my bike out of the car's trunk and assembled it in the driveway. There was no sign of Ward, but he had written. "Will be back in a jiffy." Where he'd gone or how long "a jiffy" would be was unclear.

Time to get to work. I pedaled the long, flat roads that Invasivore had instructed me to look for fishers—you weren't supposed to say fishermen anymore—and to approach them casually before making my pitch. I passed overgrown houses, abandoned churches, and recently mown family graveyards. Lake birds called out overhead, and the sun bore down into my skin. You could really ride out life in a place like Reedville, talk, and act like it was still the old times. But it was no longer the old times.

I saw some men fishing from the local pier, and I biked closer to them, but they were deep in conversation. Who was I to interrupt? I went home.

I paused on the side of the road to respond to the text from my Invasivore coach. "How many converts today?" she asked.

"One," I typed.

"The day isn't over yet!" she wrote. I'd never met her face-to-face. My coach was a robot, for all I knew.

Ward was organizing some heavy ropes underneath the house when I biked into the driveway.

"Afternoon, sailor."

"Afternoon." I hopped off and rolled my bike to a shady spot, leaning it against one of the house's stilts.

"Did you hear about the storm coming in?" he asked excitedly. "It's still three days out and just a tropical storm, but it could intensify. Some are thinking it will cut in near Morgantown, which would give us some big rain this way."

"I didn't know," I said. "I've been a little checked out the last few days."

"That's to be expected, sailor." Wade's eyes were brighter than they had been last night. "But there's so much to do around here. I might need your help with some plywood later if the forecast holds."

"Sure," I said.

"For the windows," he added. He removed his sweat-stained cap and brushed his hair back out of his eyes. "This is when it gets exciting. This is when we can really start to feel something again."

That night I could hear Wade moving around the house. I was sure he didn't sleep.

I didn't sleep either. I felt grief, genuine and overwhelming, something I've delayed for many years, sweep over me. I curled into a fetal position and gritted my teeth, letting negative emotions seep in and settle.

In the morning, I made a bitter, strong cup of coffee and went out on my bike again, swigging from my thermos as I pedaled. Fuck, I said to myself, over and over again. I felt melancholy. Why? I don't know.

This time I biked to the marina, where several people were fishing. Three men and one woman—each a few feet down from the other—had cast out. I walked up to the first man I saw. He had a white plastic bucket by his feet, and when I got closer, I could see a few inches of water inside.

"Excuse me, sir," I said.

"I've already given my soul to Jesus," he said quietly. "You can try someone else."

"It's not that," I said, my cheeks flushing red. "I just wanted to talk to you for a moment about the Red Lion."

"Did you say, Red Lion? The fish or Andy "Red Lion" McCarthy, who's running for Mayor? I don't care for either, by the way, especially the guy running for the Mayor's office."

"Did you know you can eat them?" I asked. "The fish, not the man running for office, and that it helps save native fish."

"Like swallowing poison, I'd guess," he said.

"The white meat is just like hogfish."

"Excuse me," he said, turning to me, "but I can't talk to every college girl with a mission these days. I'm going to get back to my fishing if that's all right with you."

"I understand," I said. Humiliated, I walked back to my bike. I knew my coach at Invasivore would be disappointed in my conversion numbers. Maybe I'd inflate them a little. That idea came from my fear of failure more than my desire to earn the conversion points required for the purple Invasivore hoodie and water bottle.

My dad used to say that he didn't fear failure, but I think that's because he came from an unbroken home and plenty of money. He'd never had to experience it, not the real kind.

When I got back to the lake house, sweaty and sad, Ward was there with a newly buzzed haircut.

"I went to the barber. Great guy. A hundred years old. Can't see well, always has a country-western film going on the television. I never let him do a full shave because—you know—he might cut something important." He touched his neck.

"It looks nice," I said.

"You have to stay prepared," he said. "Speaking of—we should nail the plywood on tonight."

"Sure thing," I said, following him inside.

"How's your work going?" he asked, handing me a beer.

"I'm no good at it," I said, feeling miserable.

"That's to your credit, you know."

"How so?"

"It's not honorable work," he said, his face suddenly growing serious. "You're out there trying to tell someone else how to live. You're trying to tell these poor folks how to fix a rich folks' problem. Do you know what it takes to catch a Red Lion? A spear, or a net and a Kevlar glove. It's not on the folks around here to eat the Red Lion nobody else wants. It's not on them to make it right for everybody else." He was practically leering at me. I stepped backward.

"It's to help protect native species," I said. "A grown Red Lion can demolish an entire ecosystem in days."

"It's more than that," he said. "It's always more than that."

"If you hate the idea, then why do you rent out your room?" I asked, feeling defensive.

"I don't mean to come on so strong, sailor," he said, wiping his brow and gathering himself. "It's just that guilt is all around us, you know? All around us."

He was carrying a hammer, and I felt uncomfortable. I also knew he was right.

"You should probably get out of here in the morning," he said, fishing for something in his toolbox. "Not because I don't like your work but because the storm is going to come in, and it will be hard living out here for a bit. You should evacuate before they say to. The traffic gets awful."

"I'll do that," I said coldly.

That night I packed up, having imaginary conversations with my mother. I could see my mother packing her station wagon, not able to take one more day with my father and me. We were holding her back from the life she wanted to live with powders and perfume. With freedom.

When you worry nine days out of ten that you aren't any good, that you can't keep people in your life, the anxiety plays on loop. It's a never-ending story. It's the snake biting its tail.

I woke to a strange darkness. Disoriented, I checked my watch to see that I'd slept in. It was ten minutes past nine. I realized Ward had boarded the windows and blocked the morning light. I had slept through his hammering.

I loaded my car with my belongings. There was no sign of Ward. I walked from the front of the house onto the wooden boardwalk to look at the lake, which was now kind of emerald-looking underneath the darkening clouds and rogue rays of light. The water was wild and white-capped.

I stopped at the bait shop on the way out of town for some coffee.

"Is he out there already?" the cashier asked, the same woman as before.

"Who?"

"Ward."

"Where would he be in this weather?" I asked, thinking she meant on his boat.

"You still don't know?"

I shook my head. She lowered her face as before. "He ties himself to the front of the pier when the storms come in."

"What?"

The cashier shook her head. "Yes, ma'am. It's hard to believe, but sure as rain, that's what he does. He ropes himself onto one of the pylons, and he just takes wave after wave to the face, sputtering and half-drowning himself and whooping in delight."

"Are you kidding me?"

"It's an awful thing to see," the cashier said. "Just awful. The Weather Channel filmed it once. Drove his mama nuts when she was still alive. He said he was doing it to make amends."

"For what?"

"For his family owning all that land and enslaving people. That was almost two hundred years ago, his mama would tell him—but he wouldn't listen. Like he was some sort of Catholic out there, punishing himself for the crimes of others."

I paid for my coffee and took it back to my car. I sat in the driver's seat for a long time. I could picture Wade out there in the wind and water, like a strange figurehead on a ship, mouth open, the water pummeling his face and stinging his eyes.

"I just don't think that's how asking for forgiveness is done," the cashier had said on my way out.

But I'd never met anyone who really knew how to do it.

I made a U-turn and drove back to the pier. I guess I wanted to see if it was true.

I heard Ward hollering before I got close. I held onto the edge of the railing and looked down at the top of his drenched head. The rain was persistent and fierce, but there he was, soaking wet and roped to the wooden piling. The rope wound around his chest and hips, and his legs dangling in the water. When the lapping water came—and it was breaking all over the place—it crashed into his face. He sputtered and whooped, in some sort of altered, if not ecstatic, state.

It was horrible to see, and I regretted bearing witness to it. I wondered if I was somehow responsible for his well-being. I turned back to my car and called the police. "We know about that one," the dispatcher said. "There's not much we can do, legally speaking if he doesn't want help and isn't endangering others."

"He's going to die out there," I said.

"Hasn't yet. And, honey," she added, "this is off the record, but sometimes you just have to let people like that go. If he wants to drown himself, I'm not sure we can stop him." The line went dead.

I spent an hour sitting in my car, rain hitting the windshield.

I went back out to the edge of the pier. Spray from the lake waves came up over the railing. I was scared. "Ward! Get down from there," I yelled. His body was more still now, with less fight in it.

He took out a knife and cut his ropes, plunging into the water below.

I gasped.

His head rose above the water. He dove under and came up again a few feet away. Eventually, he came up just before the water took him to shore. He crawled up on all fours.

I ran to where he was lying on his side, almost fetal.

"Hi, sailor," he mumbled.

"What the hell are you doing?"

"Suffering," he said plainly. "And to think—what I experienced out there doesn't come close. Not to a month of what they put up with from my family. Not even a day. Can't make it right," he said, crying. "Which is why you have to do better than you're doing. You can't go around telling people how to solve your problems. You solve them. You get in this goddamned water with a spear and catch the invasive fish. You clean up the lake. You get down on your hands and knees and do the fucking work. You suffer for once."

He gagged and vomited lake water.

"You need help," I said.

"We all do," he replied.

I stood next to him, waiting for him to say more, but eventually, I accepted that he was okay. I walked back to my car. I drove out of town, past the Spanish moss-covered trees, churches, and strip malls with tanning beds. I thought of my mother painting another woman's face with rouge, driving home to an apartment I'd never seen, content.

The trick I thought was to believe in your choices. Once you let the doubt in, it ate you alive. Once you started trying to be good, you could only see how you weren't. I guess people like Ward and I finally realized that, and we'd never be at peace. And that was sort of the point.

That summer ended on a sad note. I drove home to Raleigh to have dinner with my father, who'd retired from dentistry and kept his aquariums near the dinner table. He didn't ask a lot of questions when I showed up.

"Did you ever forgive Mom?" I asked. "For leaving us?"

"Of course," he said. "That's water under the bridge." But I could tell by the blank walls of his home and the placid expression on his face that he hadn't. He'd just given up the fight and let the current sweep him along. Maybe that was why she left in the first place.

We watched the exotic fish in his aquarium while we ate pizza; they circled the tank again and again, on some awful, endless journey.

Was that a metaphor for me? Had I been chasing endlessly to make amends for my mother's actions in leaving my father? Was that what my Women's Studies degree was all about? My grades were never that good, and it was like being lashed to a post and being pummeled. No wonder I was never hired for anything related to that degree.

As to the Environmental Studies degree, the ultimate irony was that I never ate a Red Lion myself.

ABOUT THE AUTHOR

John Corral

He is an award-winning author of mysteries, thrillers, suspense, legal dramas, and westerns. He also co-wrote and edited women's stories of love and life with Tanya Angel, and contributed and edited poetry with Ian Lewis and Iris Mede.

Books by the author include WATERCOLOR EYES, THE SAD PICNIC, SERIAL SINS OF SIBERIA, END OF THE PIER, THE COLORS OF LOVE, LIFE, AND DEATH, LUST, LIES, AND LOVE, GETTING SADDAM'S GOLD, LOVE TIMES ELEVEN, THE GRISLY EFFECTS OF GREEN, DID HOLLYWOOD CAUSE THE CUBAN MISSILE CRISIS?, HIS FINAL RESTING PLACE: ELVIS, REDHEADS ARE RELENTLESS, DELPHINA: VOODOO QUEEN, 30 FLASHES OF FICTION, 15 FLASHES OF FICTION, 15 MORE FLASHES OF FICTION, MYSTERY AND MALICE, IMPERFECT KILLING, PROSECUTION MISCONDUCT, REMEMBERING DIXIE, BEYOND THERE BE DRAGONS and THE MOST DANGEROUS MAN IN THE WORLD.

Books with Tanya Angel include PARIS STREET STORIES, THE SECRET LIVES OF SMILES, THE DUCHESS, WHERE THE HEART IS, and WHEN THE HEART LAUGHS IT SHOWW AND WHEN IT DOESN'T IT SHOWS EVEN MORE.

Books with Ian Lewis and Iris Mede include FLOWING LIQUID LIFE, DREAMS OF A PERPETUAL DREAMER, EVOLVING LOVE, LET LOVE FLOAT, ORDINARY LIVES EXTRAORDINARY LOVES, LET LOVE LEAD THE WAY, REAL PASSIONS REAL LOVE, LOVE THAT CHANGES EVERYTHING, THE SENSE OF SORROWS PAST, LOVE DEVILISH LOVE DIVINE, TALKING DIRTY ABOUT DESIRE, LOVE WORTH REMEMBERING, THE PLEASURES AND PAIN OF LOVE, WHEN LOVE LIFTS YOU HIGH, and WHEN LOVE SIZZLES.

John is also the author of TWO BROTHERS, a western, 3 LIFE LESSONS, an essay, and SEEING YOU, a book of poetry.

9 798433 439153